"Reminiscent of James Baldwin, LaValle does a re-markable job of capturing the sometimes-harsh reali-ties of young people growing up in urban cities."

—*The Source*

"Like [Junot] Diaz and [Sherman] Alexie, Mr. LaValle is something of a literary renegade. . . . His language is gritty, his sensibility direct and naturalistic. An aus-picious debut—and then some."

—*Washington Times*

"Earnest . . . high-wire prose about the lower depths. The no-hopers . . . are offset by one sterling character, who sees through the destructive swagger of the neigh-borhood streets and eventually gets himself out."

—*The New Yorker*

"LaValle's work is first-rate and it reminds us that by accepting our imperfections, we have a chance to become beautiful."

—*The Village Voice*

"There's a connectedness to these episodic urban tales: They all share a similar jagged rhythm, and together in *slapboxing with jesus* they generate a feeling of convincing familiarity, as LaValle envelops us in his world."

—*Los Angeles Times*

VICTOR D. LAVALLE

slapboxing with jesus

Victor D. LaValle is the author of *The Ecstatic*, a novel. He won a PENAmerica/ Open Book award for *Slapboxing with Jesus*. He has received the key to Jamaica, Queens. He lives in New York and teaches fiction at Columbia University.

slapboxing with jesus

s t o r i e s

VICTOR D. LAVALLE

v i n t a g e   c o n t e m p o r a r i e s

VINTAGE BOOKS • A DIVISION OF RANDOM HOUSE, INC. • NEW YORK

A VINTAGE CONTEMPORARIES ORIGINAL, OCTOBER 1999
FIRST EDITION

Some of these stories first appeared or will appear, in slightly
different form, in the following publications: "chuckie" in *Code*
magazine (Nov. 1999); "class trip" in *Tin House* (Fall 1999);
"Trinidad" in *Transition* (Sept. 1999, issue 80); "pops" in *Bomb*
magazine (Winter 1999).

Library of Congress Cataloging-in-Publication Data
LaValle, Victor D., 1972–
   Slapboxing with Jesus : stories / Victor D. LaValle.
      p.   cm.
   ISBN 0-375-70590-2
   1. Queens (New York, N.Y.)—Social life and customs—Fiction.
   2. City and town life—New York (State)—New York—Fiction.
   3. Urban youth—New York (State)—New York—Fiction.
   I. Title.
   PS3562.A8458S58   1999
   813'.54—dc21   99-26222
                              CIP

Author photograph © Marion Ettlinger

Book design by Suvi Asch

www.vintagebooks.com

Printed in the United States of America
10   9   8   7   6

This book is dedicated to
Damali LaValle
and
Karen Nabisase Beckford
(1915–1982)
with love

contents

one

two

—And haven't you your own land to visit, continued Miss Ivors, that you know nothing of, your own people, and your own country?

—James Joyce, "The Dead"

one

the autobiography of
New York today

(in five parts)

raw daddy

The next morning I was still scratching my nuts, for hours; in the afternoon I called Lianne; I was fiending. When I asked for her, Ray stopped flipping through television channels long enough to whisper, —What are you thinking?

She sounded like sleep; it was a Wednesday afternoon. Outside, Brooklyn traffic was turned on: boys screamed tag or bounced balls against concrete; girls were laughing. Around here, even if it wasn't funny, girls were laughing at something. She didn't recognize my voice. Ray had the sound up, loud, and wouldn't lower it, so I was screaming. It had been some time.

—Oh, she sighed. Whassup, Sean.

I laughed. —Damn, it's been seven months, you could sound a little happier to hear from me.

—I'm sorry, she said, it's not you. Work's got me standing eight hours a day. So why I haven't heard from you in forever?

—Just living, I told her, moving my hands to emphasize the first word not the second.

—Uh-huh, sure. So why you calling me out of nowhere?

She knew. Was that the sound of construction there, far beneath her voice? —What are they building? I asked.

—No, she corrected. Tearing down.

I wasn't subtle all the time, asked, —So what's up with that yum-yum?

She laughed hard despite herself. —You're a fool, Sean, you know that?

—But that's why you love me, right? She was quiet; I cleared my throat.

Lianne seemed to be thinking about it; finally she agreed. —Tonight we could do something. I don't work again until tomorrow night.

I put up one finger, inspected the nail. Ray walked for the bathroom shaking his head. He left the set on, an airline commercial; jet engines ran loud to make their point: the most powerful planes in the sky. I asked a favor for Ray, could she bring a friend for him?

—What I look like, she snapped. A pimp?

—Nah, but come on, spread love. You know? And none of your little snaggletooth, mud-duck friends neither.

—What are you talking about? she huffed. All my girls are fly.

My coughing passed. —I need to remind you that Aysha's eye is so fucked up that if you want her looking at you you have to talk into that bitch's ear?

She stifled some kind of laugh. —It's just that one eye, damn. One thing wrong and you flip. But I'll find someone for Ray.

—That's what I'm talking about. I clapped twice.

—And don't call my girl a bitch.

I apologized. Someone parked outside was pumping a tape. It was almost winter so the car windows were up, but ignoring all that bass was impossible. I couldn't tell you the tune, just the tempo. A second after a beat, their window would rattle hard; two seconds after that, our living room glass too. I wondered how far those waves could travel. For a minute, I was jealous.

She said, —Bring a movie.

—Woman, I explained, you're going to be so into me you won't be seeing straight, so forget a flick.

—Unless you had a dick transplant you better bring all types of things to distract me. Her laugh was loose in my ear.

I hung up after our good-byes, then went to the television and ran my hand over the screen. My palm came up gray with dust; electricity sparkled against my skin. I got some paper towels, glass cleaner, sprayed it on and wiped the tube down. Then I did the sides and back. I walked to the bathroom door, knocked for Ray. The toilet flushed as I knocked again and he came out, irritated.

—What man? What?

I paused. I pointed. —You didn't wash them hands, Ray.

—Man, Ray sighed, used to me. Leave me alone.

—That's why you get no ass, I told him. You go to hold a woman's hand and your fingers smell like shit! I paused so he could think about this. We're going to Lianne's.

—Not me, Lone Ranger. Ray swung at me, playful. You're on your own. Remember the last woman she set me up with?

—What? I laughed. She was willing, right? And you know you don't come across charitable girls that often.

Ray yelled, —She took her panties off and my eyes started to tear up!

—Well, you shouldn'ta been trying to eat her out.

—Sean, I wasn't even in the room.

He got me, Ray always did. That face he made was perfect, like someone had jigged him in the gut. I held my side, fell back into the couch. We had such a small apartment. It was long and thin, got wider at the end, here in the living room; the place was shaped like an extension cord.

When I opened my eyes Ray was at my face, behind him our boy Trevor. Now we were supposed to call him Knowledge, but when you've seen a boy, at thirteen years old, cry for his stolen Lego, you will never be able to call him Knowledge. The best I could manage was to use the first initial. —Peace to the Gods. I smiled at K.

He nodded approval, said, —What up, Sun?

I had fallen out on the chair in my room after making a quick trip to Harlem for some clothes. Because my work schedule was funny I had the habit of checking the date every time I woke up. See, today in 1908 the first factory-built Model T was completed. One of the benefits of working at a Ford dealership: free fun facts printed on your complimentary calendar. Henry had taken the car on a hunting trip to Wisconsin.

Ray left my room, in the back end of the apartment, wound through the kitchen, which came next, down the little hallway and into the bathroom as K and I walked. Ray had his towel and his soaps. K stopped us in the kitchen. Leaning in close, I whispered, —Man, that kid, he got like two different shampoos, a soap for his body, gel for his face. A fucking loofah pad.

K, at the fridge, opened it, stuck his big-ass head inside. —Ah-hah. Ray man, he called out, Sean is making you sound like a bitch.

But Ray already had the shower going. He thought I

7

didn't know, but he wasn't in yet. He did this every other morning, sitting on the toilet filing down his toenails. K's magic nose had sniffed out the bowl of hard-boiled eggs Keisha had made for me. His big hammy hands were all over them. While he hunted I got out a broom and swept, reaching the long yellow bristles down the hidden side of the fridge, around the oven, underneath the cabinets, pulling out all the secret bits of fallen food, paper and dirt. When I found a dime layered in dust, I threw it at K; he'd been foraging for too long. He didn't get angry. He said, —Turn on that radio.

There was one by the sink. K twirled his hands like a band leader, getting me to raise the volume. Good, now louder, he gestured. He said, —Brooklyn is amped today.

—For what?

He shrugged. —When you ever known this place to need a reason? Shit is just hot. Niggas are out and girls are, he stressed it, everywhere. It's like summer.

—That's why I'm staying in until dark, I said. Everyone starts acting up on days like this.

K dragged me into the living room, single file in the hall, his other hand carrying the food, pointed out the windows. —Nah, you gotta come build with me today. Gods are out there, right now, so much science getting dropped they're creating new worlds and shit. Universes. I got to remind you? All this shit you see before you, we made. You don't want to be a part of that?

I rolled my eyes; the T.V. was still shouting, fighting with the radio I'd left on in the kitchen. Plus Ray was singing while he washed, no shame, like how hard he sang made up for how bad. —I don't want to hear this shit today, K. I laughed at him, but who was I fooling? I loved it; I was ready to be convinced.

K could see this. He said, —You seen how many times Osiris got shot by the cops? Like forty-one.

I laughed. —Even these crazy-ass New York cops couldn't get away with that much.

He shrugged. —It was a lot, forty-one, fourteen. They shot him and he didn't die, motherfuckers told me he didn't even fall down. You tell me, what normal man's going to walk away from that? He has to be God manifested on Earth and that's what I am and that's what you are. Come to one cipher and build, just listen to the brothers and you'll believe.

Whenever I was ordering a new rearview mirror for a '92 Escort, I wanted to hear K's speeches deifying us again. If he wasn't around I'd tell them to myself. Then, if I was feeling really charged, I'd shut my eyes, had faith that if I could think of enough good things to do I'd be God when I opened them again. I'd always start small: the complete Sherlock Holmes series with Basil Rathbone and Nigel Bruce would run on channel 13 every day; I wouldn't be going bald anymore; the rent for everyone on our block paid for the next twenty years; more trees would grow through the concrete;

Ray would actually get to be an airline pilot. Each time it failed I didn't lose enthusiasm, I just hadn't dreamed up anything big enough. To be God you had to think larger.

K looked out the window. —Only thing that'd keep people calm today is clouds.

He gave me an idea. I shut my eyes. I waved my hand and thought, Rain; nothing happened. I shrugged. K started telling me something else, that Keisha knew I was cheating, that she was tired of it. I sat down, trapped again by earthly pressures.

—Where'd you hear all this? I asked.

—Her cousin.

—Alice.

—Nah. He smiled. The other one, Ayanah.

—Since when you been tight with her?

—Since she's been getting the essence of the God! K squeezed at his dick. He laughed and me with him.

—You're hitting that? I thought it was you and Alice? And you're trying to talk to me about being faithful?

He shrugged. —The God must spread his seed.

—See that, I said. Even the righteous brothers are wack.

He sat up. In his open mouth I could see the food being chewed. —Don't kid yourself, so are these women. They both have men, but look, they still come to me.

—That's real deep, I said.

—Don't roll your eyes, K protested. I'm dropping bombs and your mind can't handle it.

—Most you're dropping, I pointed out, is those UPS packages while you're working.

As soon as I stepped out these two were all over me, Ray being loud, —Damn! And I thought I took a long-ass time. Someone had turned on the fan, set it on the sill in the living room where those two sat. It was September. Cold air lanced our apartment, strong enough it might have peeled paint loose, blown bugs from their corners. I was in my towel, still wet. Between them sat the bowl of eggs my girl had made for me; they had been reduced to nothing but their grayish-white shells in a messy pile.

—Man, K said, put your shirt on. No one here wants to see your scrawny chest.

—You dream about this shit right here, I said, pointed to my pecs, flexed my arms.

—Damn Sean, K said. You been working out.

I got thrown but he seemed serious. —Well, I been doing push-ups.

They turned to each other, started laughing. K hopped up, flexing. —Well, I been doing push-ups, he said, sounding like a faggot. Our living room wasn't worth much, the ceiling creaked if you bumped into the light that hung down on a wire.

—What's your cousin's name? I asked Ray.

—Ramon?

—No, no, Chocolate or something. I pointed to my face like that might give Ray a better idea.

—Yeah. Cocoa. You got something to tell me about my cousin?

—Not him, his boy who I see all over, all fucked up.

Ray nodded. —I know who you mean, that kid is bad news.

I scratched my head. —I saw him when I bought some pants for tonight, uptown, hanging on to a phone booth like he was going to die if he let go. He was looking rough. I was standing right next to him.

Some people were always reminding you how close you were to falling off. The thought of him put a little fear in me. I took the phone down to my room and called Keisha. While it rang I folded the clothes I'd washed yesterday. Some of them were still a little wet and this pissed me off because I'd spent a whole hour with them in the dryers. Instead of hanging them out to dehydrate I creased them up and put them in their drawers. I saw this as some kind of punishment. They'd smell a little when I took them out, the fabric would wear out sooner and it would be me who'd pay for it, but I couldn't stop myself. I shoved them in like they were headstrong children determined to do their own thing. I slammed the drawers closed like I was locking the clothes in a room. Keisha's mother answered. —Hello Miss Bonyers, I said.

—Oh, hi Sean.

I laughed. —No one's too happy to hear from me today.

—Keisha's not here, she exhaled. She turned her mouth from the phone but I heard the light pull on a cigarette. Her voice was soft, showed no sign of the good thirty years she'd been doing that.

—Do you think she'll be back soon? I asked.

She considered it. —Keisha's in class right now, I think. At the college.

I nodded, looked around the room for my pick. —Could you tell her I called?

—Sean, you know she'll be graduating in two years. From college, I'm saying. She deserves something good. You understand what I mean?

We'd known each other for a long time. When I was moving into this place, after high school, she and Keisha had helped me pack some things. Keisha and I had just been friends then. Her mother told me it was a good thing for a man to get out someway when he turned eighteen.

—I know what you're telling me Miss Bonyers. Keisha could do better.

She didn't even inhale again for thirty or forty seconds. —No, Sean. You didn't hear me. That's not what I meant.

I sat quiet. Soon she said, —I'll tell her. Can she call you tonight? Will you be around?

I stood, walked to the window. —No, I said. Me and Ray are going out.

—Well then, Miss Bonyers said and left it at that.

K broke out and then we made the trip. It was a train first, just to get us out of Brooklyn. In Queens we rode a bus with no heat, people huddled up in their clothes. I tried again, eyes closed, and decreed that no one would ever go cold, but as before, I guessed my scope was too small. When the bus dropped us off, we were two blocks from Lianne's building.

—I just thought of something. I asked Ray what that was. Didn't bring no condoms for my joint, he explained. I totally forgot. You got any I could use?

—Nah duke, I didn't bring any.

—What you going to do? he asked.

—Like always papa, raw daddy.

—For real? He laughed like he was shocked. You do that shit a lot?

—Nah, just with Lianne when I see her. And Keisha. We walked toward the right building, but here in Lefrak City each one looked like the others, tall and light red brick, curved driveway out front, parking lots only for people who'd signed a lease. All the stores had bright signs, for Chinese food, for liquor, so much light I bet you could see us from the moon.

—Keisha, I said, that's my heart, so you know she's gotta feel me. Plus I want her to drop my seed.

Ray was dipping through his clothes for the fourth time, in case he'd just misplaced his rubbers, but all he found were breath mints and three D-cell batteries. He was always bringing things home from Radio Shack by mistake. Once it was a battery tester, for cars, hand-held; he'd gone through the apartment, putting the two little tongs to anything and testing for a current. He even tried the living. A cat from next door had none. I'd told him it was stupid, but in bed with Keisha one day I had her attach them to my pointer fingers, just to see if it would register a charge.

—Why Lianne? Ray asked.

—We used to always use something, but it was more because I didn't want any babies with her. I don't know how, but she shot out one ugly-ass kid.

—True. He tossed a broken red pen against a fire hydrant.

—I can't take any chances, I told him. She takes the pill. I can't have some ugly kids.

—That is important, he agreed.

At the doorway to Lianne's building we stopped and stared at each other. I pressed the buzzer. —Who? Lianne asked over the intercom.

—It's me, I screamed loud so she could hear. The

door buzzed and Ray grabbed it. Everything around us was electric, powerful. No one could have told me that we weren't divine. I'm coming for you, I promised into the speaker.

—Get your ass upstairs, she said. We dying up here.

She gave me an idea. I shut my eyes.

ghost story

Move anywhere, when you're from the Bronx, you're of the Bronx, it doesn't shed. The buildings are medium height: schools, factories, projects. It's not Manhattan, where everything's so tall you can't forget you're in a city; in the Bronx you can see the sky, it's not blotted out. The place isn't standing or on its back, the whole borough lies on its side. And when the wind goes through there, you can't kid yourself—there are voices.

I was at war and I was in love. Of both, the second was harder to hide, there was evidence. Like beside my bed, a three-liter bottle, almost full. I rolled from under my covers, spun off the cap, pulled down my pants, held myself to the hole and let go.

Besides me and the bottle, my room had a bed, some clothes hanging in the closet, books spread out across the floor. Somewhere in that pile of texts and manifestos were two papers I had to turn in if I ever wanted to be a college graduate.

Cocoa was in the next room, snoring and farting. I listened to him, all his sounds were music.

I finished, pulled up my sweatpants and closed the bottle; inside, the stuff was so clear you could hold it to one eye and read a message magnified on the other side. I religiously removed the label from this one like I had all the others, so when I put it at the bottom of the closet with them, in formation (two rows of three), I could check how they went from dark to lighter to this one, sheer as a pane of glass; each was like a revision—with the new incarnation you're getting closer and closer to that uncluttered truth you might be hunting privately. I would show them all to a woman I loved, one I could trust; that had been tried three times already—the two stupid ones had asked me to empty them and change my life, the smart one had dressed right then and walked out. This was my proof, their intolerance, that people hate the body. But me, I was in love.

Cocoa and I had grown up poor and I was the stupid

one; I believed that's how we were supposed to stay. That's why, when I saw him on the train two months before, with his girl, Helena, her stomach all fat with his seed, I didn't leave him alone. I walked right over. I was at war too, and needed the help.

She'd looked up before he did; the express cut corners and I fooled myself into thinking she was glad to see me. —Hey Sammy, she forced out. Cocoa was working, I was sure of that; she was rocking three new gold fronts on her bottom teeth.

I asked, —You going to be a mommy?

Started telling me how many months along she was but I'd stopped listening; soon she wasn't talking. Her jewelry disappeared behind her closed mouth. Cocoa hugged me tight like when we were fourteen: me and him coming out of the crap church on the corner of 163rd, the one with neon-bright red bricks, the painted sign on the door, misspelling the most important word ("cherch"). It was when his mother died, quick, and we were leaving the ceremony, behind us the thirty more people who'd cared to come. It had been a nice day so fellas were hanging out in crews everywhere and despite them Cocoa hadn't been able to hide his crying like his father and uncles had. I put my hand on his shoulder, patted it hard like men do, but it wasn't enough. So I wrapped my arms around his neck and hugged, on the corner, like even his pops would never care: publicly. When Dorice walked by I didn't stop and she probably thought we looked gay; still, I didn't force him back and try to catch up to her. And Cocoa? He didn't push me away, he leaned closer. He hugged me like that when I saw him on the train, like there was a death nearby. He looked right at me.

—We need to chill again, I said.

The way Cocoa grinned, it was like I'd given him cash. He was small, but he had the kind of smile it takes two or three generations of good breeding to grow; the one descendants of the *Mayflower* had after four centuries of feeding themselves fruit I'd never get my lips around (the kind where fresh means just picked, not just brought out for display). It was a good smile that made people trust him, think he was going places. Helena touched his leg, but he brushed her back, saying, —I'm just getting his number.

I watched Helena's back curl like it would when the stomach got grander, the baby inside pushing out its little legs like it might kick a hole; as she sank I told Cocoa my number and he gave me his; he was living with Helena and her family, back in the Bronx.

—Wake up! I yelled out to the living room.

There was a class today. Physics, I think, but me passing that now was like a dude trying to be monogamous—impossible. Cocoa hadn't missed a lecture or seminar all year, he'd bragged about it, so the last three days he'd been with me were only getting him in trouble with the mother-to-be. When she beeped him, every few hours, and he called back, she'd say she needed errands run, but her cousin Zulma was around, and her aunt; she was just on that ultrahorny pregnant-woman program and Cocoa knew. He would say, over the phone, —You know I can't sleep with you when you're pregnant, that would be wrong. I might give the baby a dent in its head. He laughed with me when he hung up, but while they were talking I said nothing; I listened from the kitchen to every syllable; if I'd had a pen and paper nearby I would have written it all down.

He stood in my doorway. He was slim as well as short but still seemed to take up all the space. Cocoa said, —You're messing me up. That stuff from last night is still bothering me. What did we drink?

—I had a bugged dream, I muttered.

—I'd hate to hear it, Cocoa said. I'm going to make some breakfast.

My hand, I placed it against the window to see how cold it was out. It wasn't a snowy winter. When I'd enrolled at City College it had been a big deal. I'd be getting my own place. My mother and sister were against it, but when you hit eighteen they call that adulthood and a lot more decisions are yours to make. Plus, you know how it is with boys in a family of women, they won't let go. When I'd first moved in, Mom and Karen were coming by once a week to check on me, but after two years of staying on top of things, schedules, they had no choice, they let me be.

Three nights ago, when Cocoa had come to hang out, I'd made him wait outside while I got things in place: threw my pillows and sheets back on my bed, plugged everything in. I kept up with news, they were doing renovations all over the Bronx: new buildings, the parks reseeded with grass and imported trees, you could almost pretend there wasn't a past.

After breakfast, for an hour, Cocoa and I took trains up and down the spines of Manhattan. Then we stood outside Washington Square Park, on the side farthest from NYU (Cocoa's school), staring at three women he thought he knew. I was shaking my head. —No, no. You don't know them. They're way too pretty to be talking to you.

He spat, —You criticize when you get them herpes sores off your lips.

I touched my chin. —They're only pimples.

—Then wash your face.

He'd been giving me advice since we were kids. He had thought that if he just told me how to be better I could be. Age ten was the first time for either of us that I acted up: when people whispering into telephones were talking about only me, a radio announcer was making personal threats (—Someone out there, right now, is suffering and won't get relief until they're our ninety-eighth caller and gets these tickets to

Bermuda!). And Cocoa grabbed me tight as I dialed and redialed the pay phone in front of our building, screaming for someone to lend me twenty cents.

Cocoa walked and I moved beside him; we entered the park. The day was a cold one so the place wasn't way too full like summers when you couldn't move ten feet without having to dodge some moron with a snake on his shoulders or a cipher of kids pretending they're freestyling lyrics they'd written down and memorized months before. —I saw Evette the other day, I told him.

He smiled. —What are you telling me that for? Anyway, she married someone didn't she?

—Well, you staring at them three girls, I thought I'd tell you about one you actually got.

We had come to an NYU building and he told me to wait outside; he was angry that I'd brought up this woman with him trying so hard to be good; really, I don't know why I did. When I'd called him a few days earlier, it had been because I knew I needed help, but once he was with me I avoided the issue.

My hands in my coat pockets, they were full of those used tissues from the flu in March. I had planned to keep them in a pillowcase under my bed when I got better, but those were all filled with the hairs I clipped off and saved, so it was September and I had never truly healed and my hands were full of dried snot.

Maybe if he hadn't been doing so well, if his girl hadn't been so pretty, if his grades weren't soaring, if he'd been unhealthy, anything, but I couldn't confide in someone doing so much better than me. I wouldn't feel like I was asking for help, more like charity. The man he was now, I couldn't sit down with him and go through all the events in my day to figure out which thing was damning me: that I woke up every day, alarmless, at seven-forty? that I couldn't stand the taste of milk anymore? that I kept putting off a trip to the supermarket and so the cupboards and fridge were empty? that I had two pillowcases under my bed, one full of cut hair, the other full of old tissues? They all made sense to me.

They all had reasons: 1) for two years I'd had nine A.M. classes so now my body, even though I'd stopped attending, had found a pattern; 2) on campus two women had pulled me aside and shown me pamphlets about the haphazard pasteurization process, pictures of what a cow's milk does to human lungs so that even just a commercial for cereal made my chest tighten; 3) I'd dated a woman who worked at the market two blocks away, had been too open in explaining my collections to her one night, sat dejected and embarrassed as she dressed and walked out forever, so I couldn't go back in there even if it was silly pride; there wasn't another grocery for blocks, when I needed food I just bought something already made and I was mostly drinking water now (to watch a cleansing process in myself) and you could get that from a tap. And 4) it wasn't just my body, but The Body that I loved. So where others saw clippings as waste and mucus as excess, all to be collected and thrown away, spend no time on them, to me they were records of the past, they were treasures. Just tossing them out was like burying a corpse too quickly—rub your face against the cold skin, kiss the stony elbows, there is still majesty in that clay. People hate the body, especially those who praise the life of the mind. But even fingernails are miracles. Even odors. Everything of or in the body is a celebration of itself, even the worst is a holy prayer.

I found, as soon as he spoke, as I considered opening myself, I hated him again; I wanted to mention anything that would ruin his happiness. Like that, I brought up Evette and the night before it had been Wilma. Cocoa came out the building, pushing the glass door with power. Smiling.

—Your divorce come through? I asked.

He stopped, composed himself back to pleasure. —Today, a little boy was born.

—Yours? I thought it wasn't for three or four more months. I was suddenly hopeful for the pain of something premature; I could talk to a man who was living through that kind of hurt.

—Not mine. Once a week I find out the name of a baby, a boy if I can, that was born. Newspaper, radio, Internet. This kid was born today, his father already posted pictures. Nine pounds seven ounces, man. Benjamin August something. He looked healthy. It's good luck.

I laughed. —I bet that kid wasn't born in the Bronx. If he was he'd have come out coughing. One fear of every South Bronx parent: asthma. It was enough to make Cocoa tap me one, hard, in the chest and I fell back onto a parked car. His child would be born in the Bronx, he didn't want to be reminded of the dangers. I put my fists out, up. I'd been planning for this, not with him, but with someone. Had been eating calcium tablets every day, fifteen of them (student loan refund checks are a blessing), and now my bones were hard like dictionaries.

He didn't hit anymore. It's what I wanted.

Do you remember the hospital? Not torturous (well, maybe one time), no beatings though; it wasn't even the drugs; try one word: boredom. You could move around but there was nothing to chase the mind, hardly even television if you weren't always good. Just the hours that were eons sitting on a couch, a row of you, ten or twenty, no books, magazines too simple for the mildly retarded and your active mind leaps further and further over an empty cosmos, as lonely as the satellites sent to find life in the universe. But in there, at least, was when I'd realized how they waged their war, my enemies: through sockets and plugs, through a current.

We balanced on a corner as cabs passed by in yellow

brilliance. It was late morning. I noticed how much energy was on: some streetlights never went off, people passing spoke on phones and the charged batteries glowed, radios came on and stayed on, computers were being run, every floor of every building. The taxi horns, engine-powered, began to sound like my name being called; I kept turning my head; the sounds bounced around inside my body, leafing through my bastard anatomy like I was a book of poems.

He spoke but the words were coming out of his mouth now all orange. I could see them, like the cones put out on the road at night to veer traffic away from a troubled spot. He said, —Look, let's not get craz, uh, let's not get agitated. I know someplace we could hang out. It'll be real good.

The NYU banners flapped with the wind, loud enough to sound like teeth cracking in your head. And how many times had I heard that noise! Like in the last month maybe five; whenever the remote control wasn't working or the phone bloopblopbleeped in my ear about no more Basic Service and I took each instrument between my teeth and bit down, trying to chew my anger out, that rage of mine which could take on such proportions.

Thought we'd catch the 4 to 149th and Grand Concourse—everybody out, everybody home. We could pass the murals of young men painted outside candy stores and supermarkets, where a thoughtful friend might have set out a new candle, where mourning seemed like a lifestyle. Instead we took the 6 and got out at 116th, walked blocks, then left, to Pleasant Avenue. My sister's home.

Cocoa saw me turn, flinch like someone had set off a car alarm in my ear, but then he put his arm on my shoulder and pushed hard, said, —Come on. Keep going. Cocoa kept pushing until we got upstairs, to the door, green, on it the numbers had been nailed in and the air had oxidized their faux-gold paint into that blackened color so familiar to buildings across our income level. He rang the bell. (Are they artificially powered?) The sound was so shrill I guessed they were part of the enemy army. Our first battle, twelve years before in the drab brown medical ward, had been so quick I'm sure they'd thought I'd forget. But I'd squirmed after they set those wires against my little forehead, so when they flipped the charge that one time, the lines slipped and burned both cheeks black; years later the spots were still there.

She opened the door. The whole place was going: television, microwave, coffeemaker, VCR. Karen was surprised to see me, but still, expecting it in some way. She was used to this.

I went to the bathroom but didn't shut the door. I filled my mouth with water and let it trickle out

through my pursed lips, down into the toilet bowl so
they'd think I was busy, held open the door some and
my ears more:

Karen: How did you end up with him?

Cocoa: I ran into Sammy a few weeks ago, gave him
my number, then he wouldn't leave me alone.

Karen: You think he's starting up?

Cocoa: I don't know what else. It's got to be. He
hasn't done this nonsense in years. He calls me one
morning and in an hour he's at my door, ringing the
bell. I'm living with my girl's family, you know? He
started kicking the door if I didn't answer. So I been
with him three days.

Karen: You should have called me or something.

Cocoa: Called who? I wasn't even sure if you still
lived here. I got lucky you and your man didn't get pro-
moted or relocated. I called your mom but the number
was disconnected.

Karen: She needed to get away.

Cocoa: Well, I know how she feels. You know I love
that kid, but I can't keep this up. My son is about to
drop in a few months. I'm trying to take care of this
school thing. He's bugging, that's all I can say.

Karen: You think you could help me out here, until
Masai comes?

Cocoa: I can't take five more minutes. I'm sorry
Karen, I am, but I can't be around him no more. I'm
through.

I listened to him walk to the door, open and shut it quietly. That thing was a big metal one, if he'd just let it swing closed behind him it would have rattled and thundered, so my last thought of Cocoa was of him being delicate.

Washed my hands and crept out, pulled the door closed and left the light on so she'd think I was still in there and snuck into her bedroom. On the door was the family portrait everyone has from Sears. A big poster of my sister, her husband and that baby of theirs. My niece. There was enough daylight coming in from outside that I didn't need the bulbs; besides, the light would have been like my rat-fink friend Cocoa, squealing to my sister about my goings-on.

There was a big bed in this big room, a crib in the corner, clothes in piles, just washed, on top of a long dresser. I walked to the crib and looked down at Kezia. She was wrapped up tightly, put to bed in a tiny green nightdress. Her diaper bulged and made noise when she moved. Dreaming little girl, she had dimples for laughing. I should have been able to make her smile even in her sleep.

From the hallway a slamming door, then, —Sammy? Samuel? Karen kicked into the room like a S.W.A.T. team. I looked, but she didn't have a rifle. She flicked on the light and ran to me, but not concerned with me, looked down at Kezia and rolled her over, touched her face, pulled her up and onto Mommy's shoulder. The

big light shook Kezia into crying and it was loud, torturous. I laughed because my sister had done some
harm even though there was love in it.

—What are you . . . is everything all right?

I looked at her and said, —Of course. I was just looking at my niece.

—You might have woken her up.

—Seems like you did that just fine, I told her.

Kezia turned toward me and then looked to her crib,
twisted and latched on to it, pulled at that because she
wanted back in. Karen finally acquiesced and returned
her. The tiny one watched me, remembering, remembering and broke out in a smile. You know why kids
love me so much? Because all kids are very, very stupid.

—She'll never get to sleep now.

I thought Karen was wrong. I pointed. —Look at her
eyes. She's still drowsy. Kezia was looking at me,
intently. I started rocking from left to right on the balls
of my feet and Kezia mimicked me. She held the crib's
rail to keep her balance but when I leaned too far right
she followed, tipped over on her side, huffed, grabbed
the bars and pulled herself back up to try again. She
made a gurgle noise and I returned it, she went louder
and I went louder, she screamed and I screamed; Karen
flopped back against her married bed, holding her face,
laughing.

My hands went around Kezia's middle, then I lifted
her up as high as my arms would allow, brought her

belly to my mouth and bit her there. She kicked her feet happily, caught me, two good shots right in the nose; that thing would be flaring up later. But she laughed and I did it again. I dropped her down two feet, quickly, like I'd lost my grip, and across her face came the look that precedes vomit, then a pause and like I knew it would, laughter.

Put her back in the crib and we returned to yelling, added movements with our hands and feet. Whenever I threw my palms in the air she did the same, lost her balance and fell backward; she lay there, rocking side to side so she could get some momentum for rising. I tickled her under the chin. We did it like this while Karen left the room and returned (repeat three times). Finally Kezia sat, watching me. I twirled in arms-open circles and she still had enough energy to smile, but not much else, and then she didn't have energy enough even for that and she watched me, silent, as she lay on her back, then Karen had to tap my shoulder and shush me because the kid was sleeping.

The lights were still on: around the crib there were pictures taped up. Of our family and Masai's, all watching over; the picture of me rested closer to Kezia than all the rest, but in it I was only a boy. Looking at my crooked smile I felt detached from that child —like we could cannibalize his whole life and you still wouldn't have tasted me. Every memory would someday make the catalogue I kept in my room, eleven small green notebooks.

Me and Karen sat in the kitchen. She had been preparing dinner. I started making a plate. —Leave a lot for Masai. He'll be home from work soon.

I covered all the pots and poured myself some berry Kool-Aid. Karen's Kool-Aid was the only thing I would drink besides water. After I gulped I told her, —You need more sugar.

She sucked her teeth. —Masai and me decided we should still have teeth when Kezia gets to be seven. Karen finished her rice. You look awful, she said.

—Yeah, but I've always looked bad. You got the beauty and I got everything else.

She smacked me, gentle, across the chin. —I had my bachelor's before you had been left back for the first time. Have you thought about coming to stay with us?

—I like where I'm at.

—You need to be around your family. You're acting stupid out there.

—Whatever. I shrugged. You don't know what I'm doing.

—I can see what you're not doing: washing, changing your clothes. Probably not going to class.

—Man, I said. You don't understand subtlety. You've got to bring these things up cool, easy, otherwise you'll close all avenues of communication.

That's how long she paused, watching me. Then she went to the fridge, found a green plastic cup. She put it on the table, sat, sounded stern, —How about you take the medication mixed with something? You still like it with orange juice? I'll make it.

I looked at the cup, the white film on top, that clump and beneath it the actual Tropicana Original. There had been plenty at my apartment, taken regular for two years, on my own. But someday you want to rest. —How about you put some vodka in there?

On top of the fridge Karen had left a Tupperware bowl of the boiled egg whites she'd been cutting up for her next day's meal. Even in the light blue bowl they seemed too bright. She wasn't kidding around. —Drink it. You told us you would. You were doing so well.

—It makes my head feel like rocks.

—But at least it keeps you thinking right. Just drink this cup. It'll be a new start. Come on.

See, but I was supposed to take that medicine twice a day, every day. She wanted me to drink this one glass and everything would go right but you can't dam a river with just one brick.

I said, —Karen, you can't stop the electric soldiers.

I was twenty-two years old and Karen was thirty. How long before it's just frustration in her, screaming to get out, wishing whatever was the pain would go away.

—Can you? she asked.

Blissfully the goddamn fridge worked, I could hear its engine going, regular like a heartbeat, mumming along and I was so jealous. When I got up she draped herself across the table, spilling the juice and the orchids she had in a vase, the ones her husband had bought two days ago, purple like lips too long exposed to the cold.

It was lucky Masai was at work. I was much bigger than Karen and I could simply pluck her off my arm and leave, but if Masai had been there it would have gotten louder, the trouble in this kitchen would have been contagious, contaminating the living room, the bathroom, their bedroom. We would have been all over the place. But at some point, as I was tugging, she let go. She could fight harder, she had before. Her hands fell to her sides; she opened the door for me.

I had other people I could have seen, but I kept forgetting their addresses. I might have passed four or five out on Malcolm X Boulevard. Later, I walked by the mosque, the brothers in their suits and bow ties selling the *Final Call*; I wanted to buy one, help them out; walked over to a short one in a gold suit; he pushed me a paper like it would save my life. —Only a dollar.

—And what do I get? I asked.

—You get the truth. All the news the white media won't show you.

I leaned close to him, he pulled back some. —You don't know that all this stuff is past tense? I asked.

Now he looked away, to his boy at the other corner, in green, white shirt, black shoes, talking with two older women; each nodded and smiled, one brought out her glasses to read the headlines. —So you want to buy this or what? My friend held it out again, the other twenty copies he pulled close to his chest. I could see on his face that his legs were tired.

But for what would I be buying that paper? Or if a Christian was selling Bibles? Name another religion, I had no use for any. I wanted to pull my man close, by the collar (for effect) and tell him I knew of a new god, who was collecting everything he saw around him and stashing it in his apartment on Amsterdam Avenue; who walked home from the 1 train stealing bouts of Spanish being spoken in front of stores and when he came home prodigiously copied them down; who stole the remnants of empty beer bottles that had been shattered into thirty-seven pieces, took the glass and placed it in his living room, in a jar, with the greens and browns of others—in the morning he sat there and watched the fragments, imagined what life had come along and done such destruction.

Instead I walked backward until I got to a corner, hugged myself tight against a phone booth with no phone in it as the people swam around me and ignored everything but the single-minded purposes of their lives. After an hour was up my brain sent signals to my feet: move.

I stood in front of my apartment again, had a paper to hand in. Go upstairs and slide it in an envelope, address it to the woman who led my seminar on black liberation movements. The one who lectured me only when I missed class and never remembered to mark it in her book. The one who had assured me that if I wrote it all down this mind would be soothed, salvaged. One Tuesday (Tues. & Thur. 9:00–10:45 A.M.) she had pulled me aside when lessons were over, confided, —These days, the most revolutionary thing you can be is articulate.

I had told her honestly, —I'm trying. I'm trying.

I touched the front door before opening it. I'd been struck by the fear that the building was on fire; a church and a mosque had been burned recently. In the secret hours of night they'd been turned to ash and in the daylight their destruction was like a screaming message to us all. Had the door been hot I would have run farther than I needed to, but it was cold so I walked in.

The elevator was still broken. I had ten stories to climb; my legs felt stiff and proud. I moved effortlessly until I reached the sixth floor and Helena stopped me. She was with her girls, they were coming down the stairs. As pregnant as she was I knew the climb couldn't have been easy, but the look on her face had nothing to do with exertion. It was all for me. —I was coming to talk to you Sammy, she said. Helena's cousin Zulma stood beside me; she was so big I felt boxed in.

—You should be out looking for your man, I told Helena.

Zulma looked like she wanted to leave, bored, but was there to get her cousin's back in case it was needed. If Helena had been alone I wouldn't have had any problem kicking her in the gut and running. When she'd rumbled to the bottom of the stairs I would have crawled down beside her and in her ear asked, —Now tell me, what does this feel like? Tell me every detail.

—Why you causing so much problems? another of Helena's girls asked, but I didn't answer. Instead I told them one of my philosophies to live by. —I never tell a pretty woman I think she's pretty unless we're already holding hands.

Helena rubbed her face with frustration. —You need to leave Ramon alone. He's good when he's not around you. Her watch beeped, not loudly, but it echoed through the stairwell. Its face was glowing. Batteries gave it power.

—Have you been drafted too? I asked Helena.

—Fuck this, Zulma muttered, then her elbow was in my chest.

As the five girls got all over different parts of me I swung wild. Caught Zulma in the mouth and the first drops of blood on my face were hers. They were yelling as I kicked out with both legs. Then I was burning everywhere and I knew without looking that the off-silver colors in my eyes were the box cutters finding whole parts of me to separate. Fabric was tearing as they removed swatches of my clothing so they could get nearer to my skin. Zulma and Helena were at my face; neither of them smiled as they did the cutting. They didn't seem angry. Their faces were so still.

I grabbed and reached for something, dipping my fingers in everything spilling out of me. The colors were hard to make out in the bad light, but the stuff was beautiful and thick, it pooled. The girls rose and ran; I listened to five sets of sneakers move quickly down those stairs to the emergency exit; the door swung out and stuck, there was the flood of an empty wind up the staircase.

getting ugly

For years I hoped I'd become a beautiful man, but by twenty-five it seemed the shit was not to be. Sitting down across from me, she said, —You know, you're really ugly.

I smiled that way I do, big eyes and funny skin. —But I get pretty when the lights go out, I said, regretted it because we both knew I was lying.

She laughed then sipped from the tall foam cup of sugarcane lemonade and had to pucker her juicy lips to let the sweetness pass her jawline. She was not perfect-pretty, but she looked much better than me; the bags barely under her eyes were good.

Her girls were waiting together in a bunch like green bananas, each one firm if you squeezed and great to eat warm. They were all tight shorts and closed faces waiting for the right brother to get them open. One said toward us, but spoke at her, —Let's go, Deidre.

Deidre turned back to me. —Since I was the one who stepped to you, why don't I just give you my number.

I was glad and said so. —I'm never good at asking for the digits.

—I don't need to know that, she said.

They had closed down Riverside Drive for the Jazzmobile. Doing that to a Manhattan street always seemed like such an impossible task, like asking your lungs to stop for a few minutes, every part of this island so essential. The guy on the drums was rolling into a little solo; music was the second-best reason to come to Grant's Tomb this time of year.

Deidre wrote the numbers with flair; her name on the paper had the mark of someone who'd been into tagging up when she was younger—it was in the e's and d's. When she put the paper to me she said, —This is my number, not no pager. I was glad, I knew what it meant when a girl passed you her beeper number: you were assed out. I tried to say something smooth, but nothing was coming. When Deidre ran up on her girls, two of them looked back at me like I had done something wrong. I stared and smiled. In under a minute they'd be putting me down and laughing, but I was more than cool with that. I figured them all to be college women—Hunter, City.

At the Tomb, the Old Audience was stacked up. I found some concrete and sat my ass between two old men speaking on seeing Charles Mingus at the Blue Note, Bird before he'd thrown it all away. They were lying of course, but I enjoyed listening to them more than the sounds of people trading numbers and quick feels.

On the phone we were cool; talking for an hour, breezing by the simple early stuff. Deidre surprised me when she cut through all the bullshit to ask, —So are you just out for ass or what?

I laughed. Not that you-caught-me-type stuff, more like, damn straight. She said, —So at least we understand each other, right?

I was nodding for ten seconds before I remembered we were on the phone. —Yeah.

—You know my girls said you wouldn't call.

I corrected her. —Your girls said I was one ugly motherfucker, and that you should hope I don't call.

She laughed. —So I guess you know women pretty well, huh?

Sucking my teeth, I said, —I don't understand a thing, but I make great guesses.

—So when are you taking me to lunch?

I asked, —Me? Take you?

You could hear her back straighten. —You do have a job, don't you?

—Of course, of course. Do you? Wait, let me guess.

She listened.

—Clothes. You sell clothes.

She was applauding, it sounded distant through the phone. —How did you know?

—I saw you and your girls together, remember? That many pretty women and you either all met working at a clothing store or you're a crew of strippers.

—Strippers?

I said, —I mean that as a compliment.

—Well, that's the stupidest thing I've heard in a while.

I shrugged. —Wait till we spend more time together.

We met on a Saturday and she was looking just as great as she wanted to, which was pretty damn good. Her walking next to me as we talked and made for the train was causing people to stare and think, What the fuck is going on with these two? We got out at West Fourth, making maneuvers here and there. She asked me, —What's your job? But I was quiet because the setting sun was sending out rays like an encore performance—with a flourish and an eye toward the audience.

—Well?

—Oh me? Computers.

She sighed. —What does that mean?

—I, you know, punch in information and all that. Data entry. Log in a lot of facts for a communications company.

She said, —You were wrong the other day. Selling clothes is one job, I go to school at Hunter too.

—That's not work, I said. That's why I didn't mention it.

—You should see my classes and tell me that.

Then we were walking down the block. She stopped at those caravans of tables selling many stolen things: books, music, clothes. I half expected to find one table with twenty blends of weed laid out, but of course they were all selling that in little doses. After two blocks she was walking closer to me, getting angry. I asked, —What's wrong?

—This is why I hate getting dressed up, she said.

—Did you think men were going to be able to ignore you? You know these guys would be in your grill if you were dressed like a fucking bum.

She nodded.

—What do you mean?

—You said it didn't you?

I laughed. —How about a little modesty though? You know? Just a No they wouldn't or something like that, damn.

Her smile wasn't too wide, didn't show too many teeth, that thing should have been worth a lot of money. —But you were right, she said.

—See, that's why I talk to only one beautiful woman at a time. More than that I think I'd die. Man wasn't meant to breathe the thin air at the top of your ego.

—Yeah, she said, like you don't have one.

—But I have the decency to have no apparent reason for it.

She shook her head. —But you're a guy, that's the way it works.

We stopped at the Benetton shop, brightly lit even during the day. Most Manhattan stores had taken on the character of Manhattan the way little brothers worship the older—in imitation. They were not exactly pretty, most stores, but they were so charming, each in a way. This is not a libel, every date I'd ever had was based on the same principle.

—So, she said as we moved again. What do you do well?

—I can do plenty. I smiled. I suppose there was a leer mixed in.

She rolled her eyes. —You're not going to start talking about sex are you? I was actually enjoying being with you.

—Sex? Me? No, I was going to say I keep my apartment really clean.

She waved off my lies. We passed the skateboard kids in front of and inside McDonald's doing their thing—ten of them nursing one bag of fries. The funny guard in his deflated uniform stood three feet away, counting down each fry so he'd know when they were gone and start shouting, —Buysomethingorgetout! Buysomethingorgetout!

—Wouldn't it be great if this was how it would always be?

She looked at me. Behind her the NYU buildings were sprawled out all over concrete.

—What are you talking about? she asked me.

—I don't know. I waved my hand. All of this.

At her apartment that night she was cooking so rough that she cursed at the frying pan and sweat ran across the back of her neck. From the living room I could watch her perspire, that's how small the place was. Mine was worse; in the paper they listed the kind of apartment I rented under "charming."

Her walls were covered with white paint, almost an old egg shell's tired gray, and little else; I was glad because I was tired of people's entire interesting lives spread out like a peep show. She took a while to calm down; when she looked at me the smell of her food came like a good comforter—got me warm and sleepy. I walked toward her; outside, a train was making noise; down on the street someone was playing music, the radio balanced on a car hood. I started dancing.

—At least you dance well. But it looks a little simple.

I laughed as I worked. —You know how hard it is to make this look easy? You're witnessing magic here. I turned to her as she sliced at some green peppers; she put her back into it. Deidre laughed while feeding me a piece. As she ate some, her lips chewing looked so good I just had to take that first kiss; she put her hand on my chest. She turned her face. —Let's eat.

I sat. She set out the meal. —So you still just out for ass?

—No doubt, I said. Of course. Why?

She ate some of the fish. —I'm saying, I see you getting all sweet on me.

I shook my head deliberately. —I think you've got that backward.

—Okay, she said. Sure.

Then Deidre was on the goddamn phone with me and I had to watch the digital lines on the clock for sixty seconds, it was really two in the morning—a week since we'd had dinner at her house. I had to touch my face to make sure I was the man saying, —It's okay, when she apologized for calling in the middle of good sleep. What's the problem?

Her voice was achy, like not in a good way. She wasn't answering my question when she spoke. I told her, as I rested my foot flat against the wall, —I bet you have a sweet singing voice.

—You don't have to try and say nice things like that anymore. I already like you.

I thought, Okay.

—From my window, she said, I can see New Jersey.

—I know good people out in Jersey.

—Women?

—I know some women in Jersey, I agreed. My room in the dark was someplace different from the spot I lived in when the sun was up. In a way, I hadn't lied to her that day we met, I was prettier in the dark, or I pretended to be. When you become an adult you accept what makes you wonderful and, if lucky, what falls short. Like my face, I was still very happy with the package, but in the dark the fun is that you can be anything. Why not pretty? That was only sometimes anyway. Other nights, alone or with company, in the shadows I was a crocodile or a ring-tailed lemur. I answered before she needed to ask, No, I have not slept with all of them.

—Only fucked them, right?

—No semantics please. Most of those women have never seen me naked.

—I see, she whispered. So they're the lucky ones.

I brought my feet across the wall, left foot close to the pipe that ran bright-hot and could burn your skin quick with just a touch. As I spoke to Deidre I tested myself, seeing how close I could come without getting my toes baked. I said, —I'm a man who lives on the edge of danger.

She cleared her throat. —You are a man who puts numbers in a computer.

—Yeah, but they're big numbers. Really big.

Deidre blurted out, —My brother got his car stolen. Out in Long Island, you believe that? Long Island is where you go to get away from that shit.

I laughed, made a bad joke.

She was on the other end of the line saying nothing; I was being funny and she was taking her brother's loss to heart. She said, —So I just heard about it and then, it's pretty stupid, but I got nervous. I wanted to hear that you were okay.

—I'm fine, I assured her. I caressed the phone with my fingertip like that would calm her down. You know, from my window, I can only see three stars.

She asked, —How many did you think you would see? This is Manhattan.

I shrugged. —I figured at least one constellation.

—Okay Copernicus, she sighed.

We were slow to hang up, but in that time we didn't say more.

Wednesday and she had no classes, no work. I left early to meet her for lunch. The last thing I was doing when she told me she was free was filing report number DS-1771 from the Federal Communications Commission, it was exactly a year old, the information, that's how far behind our office was. But I left anyway and in twenty-five minutes Deidre and I were walking to a pizza shop in El Barrio; that seemed like a shame so I dragged her to Cuchifritos instead. I watched her face and the people around us; everyone looked great, even the ugly people. It's the truth, I was comparing myself to some of the worst mugs on the block and coming up short. This fact wasn't destroying me. Any man who could be unhappy walking with Deidre deserved a stoning. I was not winning that lottery.

She stopped walking and turned to me. Her thick braids were long, swinging into her eyes; the whole thing could have been a movie poster. Whatever she was about to say, I didn't want to hear it. I didn't want any of this cool shit between us now, no mood for humor. I opened my arms and pulled her close to me, held her tight enough that she might remember the grip for a long time.

When we walked into the restaurant I ordered some chicken and pork; yeah, that's right, some mother-fucking pork. I sat at the counter while she slid right to get some drinks; when she sat back down we were still quiet. Finally she said, —I like watching people walk by.

I nodded. —Me too.

It was the middle of the afternoon; so many people rushed past outside that it was hard to make one person solid, turn our attention to him. Across from the restaurant a storefront was being redone, blue canvas flaps hung down over the windows, they were still open for business. I pointed. —What kind of store do you think that is?

She was eating, but talked with her mouth full, that's how great she was. —I don't know, she said. A stationery store? Magazines?

I smiled. —Maybe, but look, it's only men going in and out of there.

—Oh, you're right. And ugly ones.

I laughed happily. —I bet you could picture me coming out of somewhere like that.

She looked at me.

—No, she said. I couldn't.

slave

Rob eats pussy like a champ.

He's on awful knees that should have been turned in months ago; they are now numb. He should be getting ready for school; tenth grade is usually the age of football teams and part-time work.

She says, —Don't stop, through those teeth so white Rob was sure they were caps when he met her in front of the Disney store in Times Square and Andre was across the street in his jacket blue like veins, gesturing to her, Rob's customer. There's a lamp on the nightstand, weak and sputtering light.

Outside the sun is a rumor; maybe in one hour it'll be up and they have been on that bed together for much longer. He has been doing the same thing continuously, except for breaks when it's understandable that muscles tire and freeze; then he drinks handfuls of cold, cold water from the sink in the bathroom.

—Don't you fucking stop.

She has soft skin everywhere and does nothing he might call work. This woman doesn't have rough fingers like secretaries who must type and dial phones all their lives or lawyers who look tired and must win every argument; not even models who are so pretty, or pretend to be, that they would never have to pay for an ugly little kid to eat their pussies. Her legs and thighs are draped over his shoulders, her ass somewhere in that space between him and the bed; he wants to tell her that his shoulders hurt, but will he?

No.

In front of Disney, Rob had moved to touch her face, but the collar of her jacket was pulled up and flopping like mud flaps. She had to speak to him through them, saying, —It's so windy out. She stepped away. —Sure, Rob said.

Then on the train they were moving fast, it was nighttime. When he asked, —So how'd you meet Andre? she pulled something invisible up between them.

After the Columbia University stop their car and all the ones trailing and leading were just mobile testaments to the lingering effects of miscegenation.

Eventually, the train rumbled and stopped and jerked forward; he touched her arm. —Let's go. In the air Spanish was being spoken. Rob took her to the same motel as his men, walked the same path; he could see his footprints in the concrete.

On the bed, backed against the headboard, her thighs ache; she rubs them, tells Rob they hurt, but he wants to laugh because he's still on his knees, afraid to stand; his body is assuring him it will not work. His mouth is a wound that should be left to heal, but there is her purse next to the bed, pregnant with bills rolled into a rock. He has four twenties, a ten and a five in his coat that she'd peeled off earlier and even in the way she tossed them to him there was the promise of much more.

He rises but his body has forgotten how to stand; he falls back against the wall and is lying there beside the door with his legs finally straight; blood is pumping and life is returning; his feet twitch as though they're being resurrected. —Come here, she says, but his hand's up, begging for some rest. Her face, for a few moments, betrays her, there is some warmth and sympathy, she does not wish Rob any pain. She does not have children. Waiting, she tries to imagine what she'd have served a baby for breakfast that morning, how she would have spoken to convey her love. You ever have a girl? she asks. That you liked, I mean.

—Why?

She shrugs. —Just wanted to know. Wanted to hear about it.

On the walk to the motel she had finally looked at him. —You are young, aren't you?

He smiled. —As young as you want. Then he ran his hands across his chin and neck and all the places where he had, just that morning, run the razor and swept away all signs that he had aged past thirteen. Later, in the room, he moved his hands down his slight neck, over his stomach, under his balls, looked at her, saying, —Smooth.

—Like a little, little boy. She said this while touching her tummy.

She sat in that room alone with him and didn't check the closet or push open the bathroom door (just in case) because she had trust packed tight in her purse next to the money and a .38. The first thing she said to him was, —I'll give you ten dollars if you let me do this. Rob took the money, then she emptied the gun, slid the barrel into his mouth. For five more dollars he let her pull the trigger twice. The hollow clicks made him giggle.

Rob had had a girlfriend, two years before; he was fourteen and she was twelve. But when he and Inca got together he lost fascination quick because already her pussy was all used up. That was how he felt and when he asked her about it she laughed, said, —You'll find out how when that asshole's all fucked up.

And she was right.

Soon she had to leave because Rob was always trying to put fire to things—like her. She broke out finally
when he set his own right foot to burning, just to make
his friends laugh. She was saying, —If you'll do that shit
to yourself, I don't know what the fuck you'll do to me.

Healing was tough and peeling skin is ugly, but
Rob's girlfriend looked worse, had that face like she
and a train had gone at it, does it really matter who
won? He was dumb and thought he could do better so
he drove her away on purpose, but who knew after that
that nights and days would just be business, business,
business?

Inca knew that even from a distance her young skin
looked withered and loose on her bones and still she
expected you to treat her nice. She demanded it. If not,
she was gone, no question.

What he missed most, she could talk this talk, knew
this language that was from somewhere before Spain
landed ships and Spanish cut out more natural tongues;
it was hard to hear her speak like that, Rob was jealous;
when she spoke, it seemed as though she had her own
good and wonderful time machine.

—Do you want to make more money? she asks Rob.

—Of course. What do you want to do?

She pulls the covers up around her like a robe. He
wonders what her sheets look like at home. —Let me
see your dick.

Everything is quiet while he pulls down his underwear, then quiet for longer. He looks down. —What's
wrong?

—Nothing. Nothing.

—Is there something wrong with it?

—No, it's not that. I just haven't seen many up close
but my husband's.

—He make his different?

—No. She scratches her stomach. No, no.

—Forty to fuck. Rob touches his legs, still not quite
alive.

—Forty?

—Yeah.

—Forty?

—Come on. Do you want to or not?

—Hey! she snaps. Don't forget who's got the money.
He can't. He says, —Sorry.

She is smiles again. —You remind me of a boy I used
to like. He had a body like yours. Do you play sports?

—Yeah, he says, moves closer. I fuck.

—Okay, she sighs. Enough talk.

—Money first. Rob exposes his palm to her face. The
four tens are smooth and new like the others had been;
he can picture her at the ATM right before she got on
the Long Island Rail Road, the honey-sweet sound of
the money flipping out in bundles.

—I have to use a condom, he says and even her blood
is glad he brought it up.

He wraps one around his dick. But what about the

times when there was nothing latex available and he used cellophane bags and then Scotch tape and then—most often—nothing? It has been sore for weeks or maybe months and could it be longer than that?

When he gets to the bed he bumps the nightstand, moves the whole thing. It seems to her that lamp will spill over and singe; she moves her hands to catch it, but he does nothing because it's nailed down, wouldn't move if something divine came in and tried to displace it. His hands are around the base of his dick, trying to strangle it so the blood can't escape. But it does.

—How long have you been doing this?

He wants to do something to her with his fists. —Long time, he promises. Wait, there it is. He comes toward her, but with each step air leaks out like an old balloon.

She says, —So is this like a cab? Even the time we're sitting still the meter's running?

He's got nothing to say, he's watching himself; keeping it stiff is like balancing a tray of dishes on one hand and walking them across a stage, a comedy act. —It's gone. Rob does not complain, his mouth and body are mostly tired of the taste and shape and force of dicks and the men that own them. Being with a woman is a treat. Rob gets down on knees, prods tongue out with fingers, stays this way for the long hours ahead.

———

In the midmorning they say good-bye. Before she leaves there is a promise: that she will call Andre, ask for him. He nods. —Don't forget my name.

—Rob, she says and it almost sounds nice.

All the money she'd paid is lodged in his underwear. As he walks away, the stiff bills cut against one leg; he walks with a hitch like some old cowboy. A two-hundred-dollar limp. But it's all for Andre. When Rob gets back to the apartment that five people share, there will be no negotiation, only Andre's underfed palm. Maybe if he's fortunate he'll be given twenty dollars, or forty, enough to buy some magazines or go to a movie, but only if the whole apartment is in a good mood; there, generosity is an occasion.

You will find ways to save yourself. This is relative: save.

Rob's been at this long enough to have radar; a crowded hall has its interested and they can find one another. Those who weathered the Holocaust have been known to find a fellow fortunate survivor at the other end of a restaurant.

Because he's tired, Rob feels bold; he is most ready for a change just before the trip home, the emptying of his coffers. The Port Authority pizza shop, on the subway level, has a court of white plastic seats and tables. Rob has spotted the man from four hundred feet; Rob has come closer to be more sure. Passes by, four times, slowing progressively, thinking: Notice, notice. But the man, he loves his pizza, soda too. So Rob passes by three more times, decreasing his pace more until, with his arms stretched forward, Rob could be Boris Karloff's mummy chasing Abbott and Costello through a tomb.

—Why don't you go away or sit down? The man finally asks, leaning back in his chair.

Rob finds speed again, comes around the short railing. Sits. —Nice to see you.

—No it isn't, says Harrold, who tells the truth. He is much too thin, you can't hide any secrets in a body like that. And his mustache is long, a U turned over his lips, hanging down. Gray. On his cheeks and neck more hair grows in, enough to unsmooth the skin, but it will never be a beard. His fingers are slim but the tops are fat bulbs. The nails are dirty. I drive a truck, he explains.

—You take a lot of coke? Rob smiles, earnestly asks.

He laughs, and the teeth are bad, dull. —Not so much anymore. I don't meet boys like this, really.

Rob nods, he loves the liars, leans forward and tries for sultry. —Then how do you meet them, really?

Harrold coughs on some crust causing clutter in his throat. —I didn't mean it like that.

Behind them are the young women and men, a few years older than Rob, standing in a long and winding cord before they buy their tickets for Greyhound buses; upstairs the same line exists for Short Line tickets and this is the painted pattern many mornings. These young people are on their way back to college, the names stitched across their sweatshirts Rob's first, best clue; some are with their parents, but most are with the people they call Honey or Sweetheart, then kiss quickly and, with a jumble of sad and happy, watch the bus make concrete the distances between them. Rob turns back to Harrold. —Leaving isn't always sad. It can be a good thing.

Harrold doesn't understand he's being given a hint, a suggestion, but he nods because he is polite enough and Rob is pretty, which always coaxes manners from the worst of men. He asks, —So, how does this work? You want to go to the bathroom or something?

There is an information booth, empty, twenty feet away. The lights are off, glass on all sides, there is no mistaking the vacancy, but people still walk to it, stand there expectantly. As though their need for something is enough to make it appear. As though you don't have to put in any effort. Rob knows better, you have to work things. —We could do that. If that's all you want.

—What else? Harrold asks, touching his pocket. You selling vacuum cleaners too?

Anxious. Anxious. Rob does not want another night in the room he shares with three other boys, the way wind seeps through the window frame despite the black tape Rob has put up as insulation. He is desperate. He offers, —I can cook.

Again, Harrold's coughing. He's a shy one, it won't

work to be dirty or prurient, that will not coax charity, affection. Women are used to this, the way they sometimes have to set it all up before their date will reach out and hold hands. It can be playful, it can be infuriating: leaning close, smiling often, brushing near, grabbing elbows. But it can be done. Rob says, —My biscuits are nice. My mother taught me how to make them. Or cinnamon French toast, I know how to do that too.

Harrold's legs are long and, while his upper half leans back, far, they reach forward. He is conscious of it, but not in control. They would not listen if they could. He touches the insides of his boots to the outsides of Rob's sneakers. Harrold says, —I live alone. But he had not meant that to come out; internal monologue, not for Rob. Harrold, embarrassed, sits up quick, pulling his feet back from their foreplay. Someone younger, less experienced, would have jumped on the admission, but Rob pretends he hears nothing. He says, —I want to get some soda.

—I'm not paying for it, Harrold burps, quickly, like he's caught Rob at something.

Rob laughs easy. —I don't want you to. I have money, I just want to know if you'll stay here.

—And if I won't?

—Then I'm not moving.

Harrold dips his head. —Sorry, I didn't mean anything. I'll wait.

Rob walks, careful not to wiggle or strut, so when Harrold looks, and he will look, he'll see a boy, with a gentle limp. Rob does not romanticize it with emphasis.

—I'm not gay, Harrold explains when Rob returns.

He nods. —Me neither. Rob reads; in other places they will eat bugs for food, the will to survive so strong; Rob understands them.

—I'm Harrold, with two r's.

—That's weird.

—Telling me? Two of anything in your name and people think you're strange. Just your name can make people call you a monster, low.

—My name's simple: Rob. Want some? He lifts the drink and gestures like it's a gift or a secret to share.

Harrold stands, walks away. Nothing said. He creeps off to the newsstand, goes around to the far end so Rob will think he's left altogether. Rob has spent some of the two hundred for the drink, just a dollar, but accounting is Andre's passion. Rob looks around, agitated, for a purse, a man not watching his pants pockets, a way to replenish that one bill. The fluorescent lights live on, unaware of what and whom they illuminate; they are just a mechanism. Rob begins to weep. He's exhausted, had really thought Harrold was it. At least momentarily, someone who'd take him in. He should have at least gone for the blowjob, that's twenty all for yourself, off the books. He gulps his soda but there is too much ice, the drink cold enough to awaken the nerves of his teeth, too easily roused. They flare, grouchy yawns. Rob eats soft things because he's brittle. He loves ice cream despite the temperature; the occasional pint of vanilla-chocolate-cookie-dough is an exercise in gratification and self-flagellation.

Harrold then returns like he wants to be: a hero.

—Why the tears? I just went to get a pack of gum.

—Oh. Rob grins. Can I have a piece?

Harrold has lied, has bought nothing. He feels stupid in front of this kid.

Rob asks, —Are you going to sit back down? He shifts in his seat as the older man comes back around. He touches his face, rubs the skin and pats down his hair because when he gets tired age grows in like a beard. What does this guy like? Young and stupid? Young and mean? All the variations, they go through Rob's computer; how to convince this man to take him along, it doesn't matter where. It begins to confuse Rob and when confused he taps his legs with his hands but knows that annoys others so he tries to stop but then only taps more. In a panic he blurts out, I can be really beautiful.

—Huh?

—You could put me in a dress. Or anything. Whatever you like. I'll make you dinner or lunch like that, dressed up. I wore makeup before, I know how to make it look real nice. I could be your pretty young wife. Rob is sobbing, biting his lip, but not yelling, it is ingrained that, in this world, you keep things quiet. I don't care, whatever you like.

Harrold finds his courage. Evaluates the boy: small shoulders, little hips, nice mouth, he will be gorgeous; and look at him, he's terrified. Abject fear can breed a kind of loyalty. And it can be arousing.

They walk near each other but not together; like the old idealized wife Rob trails back five feet, out of deference, gratitude. Upstairs they leave the Port Authority, walk until they reach the garage where Harrold hands a short man a ticket, when the car comes, a tip. Rob walks ten feet of sidewalk, then waits for the blue Chevy Corsica. When he gets in, Harrold's pants are already mostly down. Rob goes to touch him but is brushed away. —Not yet, Harrold says. Tell me something. He begins a self-caress. Tell me something bad.

When Rob started, working, was on his own, before Andre had pulled him over in Washington Square Park, asking, —You don't know what the fuck you're doing, do you? Before Kim had him posing for pictures for men in apartments and homes; before the five of them had come together, four to work (Rob, Kim, Caps and Monty) and one to manage (Andre), prior to all that Rob made money where he could, a freelance man—most often in the lovely public bathroom or pacing through Central Park in the areas under bridges, dark tunnels that hid men needy and willing to pay someone so young.

After he had made his money (however) Rob rode subways for long hours, a stretch to last days, only sometimes getting off (pick a station, any station) to find a storefront, bought ten or twenty candy bars that he would then carry in a sock he never wore (wouldn't even wipe up with it). While reriding the trains, after booty was bought, the lights above your head were hypnotic if you laid back and watched; eventually you saw the way they dimmed and brightened, dimmed and brightened (you're getting sleepy) and before this brought him into a trance, Rob would dig into his sock, that sock, and bring forth one candy bar, eat it in two bites, the sugar dancing in his system, and watch the lights some more. For a year.

The Verrazano Narrows Bridge is impressive. It costs seven dollars. The thing is all fogged up so that when they cross into Staten Island it seems like one of those enshrouded areas in movies. A crush of cars returning home like the two of them. Harrold touches the rearview mirror and twists it until he can see himself.

—You look nice, Rob assures, but the man has grown beyond some vanities. The land is green and gray, white paint divides the lanes. They take the third exit, ride along a minor curve as they merge with the traffic on Clove Road. Now Rob sees buildings: the stores in strips that could be the signs of a civilization gearing up or winding down. They pass homes in rows sitting on very slight hills, many tilted in odd directions, as though something has set them out quickly, in a rush to leave. Some children are more careful with their toys.

Harrold asks, —You want to see where the ferry comes in? He says it like this will be impressive.

Rob doesn't think he'll care but soon he's excited. Down by the ferry is the closest this island comes to being a city. Rob doesn't think this borough is dying to industrialize and overpopulate. While Manhattan often seems to cry, Colonize me! along its overcrowded pores, this whole land shrugs at the idea. At times it even turns its back.

Rob fidgets and opens the glove compartment. Various papers and empty packs of gum are crushed by a clear plastic bag of egg yolks, twenty or thirty. He pulls them into his lap. They are greenish along with the more customary yellow. They have not gone bad. Rob opens the Ziplocked top and inhales the strong smell. He takes one out, it is flaky in his hands and weak, the ball crumbles. Rob chucks it all in his mouth and chews. He licks his palm.

—That's mostly all I eat, Harrold explains.

—You ate pizza.

—I said mostly.

Rob shakes the bag. —I could make you better things than this.

Harrold grins. —I'd like that. But those are still good. The yolk is the brain of the egg. He taps the steering wheel with the index finger of the hand that steers.

—I would have said the heart, Rob says.

Harrold shakes his head. —Eggs have no heart. Just the shell, the whites and those. You peel away and finally get down to the real life of the whole thing. I think it's amazing really, how they planned it out so well.

—Who?

—Who? God. Don't you know that?

Rob nods along, but doesn't get it. He is pretty sure this whole egg metaphor is being taken much too seriously.

—Secession? Rob points to the visor on his side that he's pulled down to check his face, but instead of a mirror there is a sticker: silver background, black letters and a little boat at the right end.

—Secession, Harrold agrees, twists in his seat.

—I know that word, but not what it means.

—These days? Harrold spits. Nothing. Not one damn thing.

Rob shakes his head. —No, come on. What, really?

Harrold gestures with his hands for an effect, but what kind even he can't say. —It means when someone decides they want to be on their own. That they want to live on their own, in peace.

They wait at a light. Rob grins to Harrold and announces, —Then I'm in secession!

Harrold laughs loud and hops in his seat as much as he can and still drive. —That sounds good to me, Rob, real good. I don't have much food in the house. You eat a lot?

—At least a little.

—Yeah. Okay then. Harrold pulls his Corsica in front of a convenience store. The only move he makes is to pull his pants down again. It is daytime. You can do better than that last one. I don't care about you riding on trains. You want some food, give me something worse. The street, tell me about that kind of stuff. He holds himself in anticipation.

—You could save it, Rob had been told before they got in the car.

This was so long ago. He doesn't really remember their faces, he's not good with those, not names either, but give him maps to decode, addresses—anything with numbers. If he knows to memorize it, then he can say it to himself four times and the information will never be forgotten.

—You could save it, Rob had been told before the three of them got in the car. You keep the atlas.

He held the map, got the front seat. Next to him the driver was his father, checking to see if they'd packed properly. It was as if they'd been evicted, all Rob's things were in two boxes. A day later they found a small blue lake, tossed in Rob's pants, shirts, socks and books; his dad promised, —Forget all those old things. We're going to get you better stuff. In the back, his mother had brought sandwiches.

In the navigator's seat, Rob was Direction Man, calling out the proper interstate numbers, the right exits. They had said to him, over a dinner of thin chicken, bread, in a rest-stop McDonald's, —Okay then, you choose where we go. And Rob had, for two nights, surveyed the atlas of the entire country with painful delicacy. He'd traced the red lines leading from home to everywhere; finally he came to his parents and said, —Let's go to New York, they make Sno-Kones there.

To pass time they played a game: after eating, his father and mother climbed in the car, that old thing, and told him to stand there and count to one hundred. When he began, the car got going, off, away, gone. By forty-five, the first time, Rob was quivering, at eighty-two he was in tears, but they were back by ninety-seven, hugging him, caressing his little head. Laughing. Telling him that he looked silly. —Stop making a big deal. We were just playing. Each next place they made him count higher, one hundred twenty-five, one-fifty, three hundred.

It did get fun to wait and see how close to the number they could come. At four hundred fifty they were late and Rob kept counting, he got to five hundred before they were back. His dad told him, —We were seeing if you were going to cry! and pointing at him and grinning. And Rob said, —Nah, I wasn't scared.

—You could save it. She pointed to the map again, before only two of them got back in the car. Rob stood on a block he'd know as years went by, in Manhattan, with buildings that go up and up, then more. They had pressed the atlas in his hand, they had started the car, they'd said, —Okay, count to one thousand. He stopped at one thousand four hundred ninety-one. He waited.

Harrold gets out. Rob has cleaned a mess with his shirt, which was off and is now on again. He flaps it with two fingers, the window open, so the cool air can come in and dry things. Harrold returns, opens the car door and takes his keys out of the ignition. Rob feels light-headed and when he feels like that he is the prettiest thing on two feet, including all those agile birds. He is giddy. In his back pocket, folded into a thick square, is the cover of the atlas he'd been given, the rest ripped in a rage by Andre one afternoon. He takes it out, holds it over his mouth like a CB radio and speaks into it like there's a direct connection to his family. He believes they want to hear from him. He assures them, —Harrold seems nice.

Harrold is back at the car door, two plastic bags in one hand as a cop car pulls in two spaces away. There are no vehicles between them. Harrold pops the unlock button, then opens the back door. He doesn't notice the officer. Rob looks over to the fat young man in his uniform sitting with his head back, hat off, engine still on, both idling; the rims are filthy and the bottom four inches of both doors he can see. Harrold gets in the car but has forgotten his keys. Finally he notices Rob intently staring and runs back to the store, but slow enough to avoid suspicion.

Eventually the officer looks left, to Rob, who still watches. The young man nods and smiles but Rob sits cold-faced and unwavering, long enough for the cop to shrug, open his car door and walk inside. He and Harrold do not pass each other on the way out, they are in the store together. The place has a fruit stand but displays only tomatoes and bananas. The bananas are divided evenly between too green and too brown. The tomatoes are smallish but not meant to be; they look hard, even from the car, and it is doubtful those things have a swallow of cool pulp in them. They are sour.

Rob decides that whoever exits first, Harrold or the cop, he will go with him. He does not love Harrold and the police can also take him someplace different from the apartment he shares with Andre and the others. A group home. He has been in them before, briefly, repetitively. Eight months ago he was in one and contacted by his family, an aunt, who told him that his mother and father were all cleaned up. At any time, he could return. She gave him their new address. At the place, his counselors gathered before him once a week with notepads, an audience, wanting to hear his whole life explained. Harrold was like this. The cop would be too, he would need to hear of Rob's days for his reports: juvenile crimes, those kinds of records. They can't get too many stories, most people, and always they demand: worse, worse. As though the more fucked-up meant the more authentic. They are slaves to this idea.

In the only letter he wrote home, Rob told himself to dispense with lying. Why make anything up? If being honest, life in New York is as mundane as anyplace else. The strangeness, the terror and joy of selling your ass, subsides. Eventually you can't remember which of the things you do would be called wrong by your mother and father now and inadvertently you'll mention that when you first started working your butt bled again and again. The only correspondence you'll receive will be from your father, saying you're an awful son for making up stories to hurt your mother. Still, he will have put forty dollars in with his harsh words. It will be a sign of his renewed goodness and love when this happens. But you, if you're Rob, will no longer be sure of those realities and will instead wonder if the money is your father's way of hinting that he wants you to come home, so he can try you out.

ancient history

I

Horse's girl was a socialist and not too pretty. They had had a kid. She was taking all his time. Me and him hardly knew each other anymore. We were months out of high school.

She learned to avoid us—when she visited we gave Horse hell and her silence. It was purely a mistake when she pulled up to Horse's crib and we were on the stoop. She had their baby wrapped tight in a gray blanket, saying good-bye to some friend who was driving; she was smiling, but when she turned her face fell.

Melissa watched the four of us: Horse, Asia, Mel and me. Except for Horse, we began laughing. I did, then Asia and Mel followed. This had become so regular it was a kind of greeting. Horse walked to her and his arm went out like a kid grabbing the side of the pool to get steadied. He dipped his head to see his son. Asia went inside to use the phone. —I thought you were going to be alone, she tried to whisper.

He said, —They just showed up. That's how I knew he was still, a little, my boy Horse: he had lied, we had been around forever.

At the stairs she trudged between me and Mel; he looked up, was going to nod because Mel was polite, his dad raised him that way. Mel was fat and dumb, but the two had no connection; Asia was fast and dumb, but no one ever tried to blame one on the other. But Mel was going to nod so I reached out and mushed his cheek to move his gaze. Even though he got mad at me, it was like I'd shaken it loose—how we wanted to act toward her—so Mel looked down as she passed.

Melissa had given a plastic bag to Horse, who carried it as tender as she did that kid. When he got to where I was on the stairs I snatched it from his hands, looked inside. She had brought a loaf of banana bread, fresh enough it was warm through the bag. I loved the smell but wouldn't inhale in front of them, it would be like approving of something. There were sheets of paper too, flyers, black ink on yellow paper, printouts stating that next Wednesday was the seventy-first anniversary of the founding of the East Side Chamber of Commerce; listed all the wrongs they'd done to the poor, the struggling. There would be a rally. This was the stuff that did it, she was a little older, a college student; quick to teach, quick to lecture. Horse would try to preach to me her thirdhand theories when all I wanted was to watch a movie. I ripped the ten identical sheets and handed them back to my boy.

Melissa asked, —Do you ever go home?

Horse laughed a little, straining to get out a sound. I looked at them. I wasn't going to hit her. I was. I said, —Horse, take this bitch back to Kent State.

He shook bad enough for both of them and I waited for him to do something. To swing on me. Imagine, if he had thrown blows over a woman, that would've been it, even stupid-ass Mel would have spit on him. I mean, I'd heard of men dying over that shit and once you're dead, what do you think, the girl mourns you for the rest of her life? Please, sooner than is fair she's fucking again. Men and women aren't that different. But Horse didn't have to decide, Melissa touched his neck and whispered, —Let's go inside. So they did.

Asia came along in a minute. Across the street and half a block right was the small space quarantined behind a tall gate. It was a grassy yard; in the center a light green metal dome popped out of the ground. Kids said it was a reservoir, but I wasn't sure. Horse would have known, but I didn't ask him too many questions anymore. Plenty times, Horse asked my opinion about some female he was spending time with, if I thought this one would cheat, if another seemed like good ass. But with this one, Melissa, she had just appeared. I couldn't even imagine where they'd met. Horse never explained.

The three of us left together; we made no noise, not even feet hitting heavy on the pavement; there was just the sound of Horse locking his front door.

2

I went with him, went in, but it was a mistake. I was out shopping for Melissa when I came around the corner and Ahab was opening the door to the recruiter's office. Marines. He was more than surprised, seeing me; he hadn't gone to the office near us. He had traveled. —Oh shit, Ahab cried when I touched his shoulder. What the fuck you doing way out here, Horse?

I pointed to the door. —I wasn't going in there. What about you?

There was no excuse coming, just his big mouth, open. You'd think I'd caught him kissing a man, he was so shocked. Ahab couldn't even move when two guys tried to get in; I had to push him back. They passed between us. I looked inside—the whole front of the place was glass; the Marines watched us greedily. I was sure that already their hands were on the sign-up contracts, ready to flash pens like knives. He explained, —I need to do something.

—Do something else, I said.

—Like what? He laughed. You know another girl with an apartment in Manhattan?

I held the door and shoved him inside; the place was spare: posters of healthy-looking guys carrying guns or swords, their hats bright as the white of a boiled egg were the only decorations; there were three desks, and behind each a smiling serviceman, one black, one white, one Latino. I was surprised by the efficiency. They had the major constituencies covered. A couch sat to the right, in front of it a small table with magazines neatly stacked. The white guy started pitching, —Well hello, gentlemen.

The black Marine looked at me. —You two here to join us?

I thought, Not me, pawn; I said, —Not me. My friend. The four of them smiled like this fact alone deserved praise. The white Marine said, —Call me Dan, to Ahab. It's good to see a young man like you ready to make some money, have some fun. Do something.

—Yeah, Ahab said. One of my boys is a Marine.

Sanford was the Marine we all knew. Each time he had leave he'd come see his family, then all the fellas. Every visit he was displaying something new. The last time had been a gray Suzuki Samurai. Everyone's parents owned cars, but it's one thing to borrow your mother's Accord and another to have one. This is not a small prize. Just Sanford had done much to make the Army, Marines, Air Force, whatever, more appealing.

—Good pussy in Germany, Dan said. Ahab nodded at this fact brought out from nowhere. Dan had a funny smile, he moved it around his face so he always looked a little stupid. It was ingenious. He wasn't intimidating that way, it made his jokes seem funnier. I wondered if that was part of recruiter's training. Dan asked my boy his name.

—Ahab, he said. He was used to the quizzical look all three Marines wore. My parents liked books.

Dan smiled. —Well, Ahab, let me tell you what fun is. Fun is running up in some pretty little Filipino girl and leaving the next day.

The Latino Marine said, from his desk, —Filipino girls. Those women are strictly fine. His nose was twisted to the left, he'd broken it a few too many times. It sat there on his face, his only medal.

The room wasn't small, so when I asked a question I had to shout. —So we spend billions just to get American boys foreign pussy?

Even Ahab, they all watched me like they were waiting to hear what was so hard to believe. Ahab was angry with me, he shook his head with Dan the way two doctors might over a patient long past saving. I shrugged. The one with the busted nose said to Ahab, —I think your friend needs a little . . . , then he punched the air twice.

Standing and smiling, I said, —That's perfect! Don't say anything else, please.

The black Marine was a clod; he was scowling at me as though I was embarrassing him. I walked outside, down the block to the store I'd come for, a Lechter's that sold better wares than the cheap imitations on Jamaica Avenue. I wanted to surprise Melissa with something, even as simple as a cutting board, just to show her I was serious about making a home. Inside the store I looked at bread baskets and salad forks. In one aisle I passed two guys, my age, unpacking boxes. One was promising that kids from Hollis were going to take care of some people in Queens Village. How many times had I been around this nonsense? Brothers from Laurelton fighting ones out of Rosedale, the same between South Jamaica and Rochdale. The fights were all the same. Queens is huge. Of all the boroughs, it is the only city to stand on its own. Manhattan pretends at self-reliance. You hear of one borough battling another, Brooklyn vs. the Bronx, like that, but here, Queens has enough of its own. We don't need to import enemies. Among ourselves we've got all the fights we can handle.

3

Horse dragged me out to Rockaway Beach. We took a bus. He looked stupid because he carried a red T-shirt the whole time, some shit balled up inside. He said it was for me. The whole way I was bugging him to let me see, a peek. But he'd always been stubborn, it's the one damn thing I'd have been happy to see change. I looked at the shirt again. —Now?

—Will you shut up?

It was daytime, a Wednesday. To get to the beach we crossed a parking lot that was empty. There were streetlamps every twenty feet, for night, but one was on anyway, burning so hard you could hear it. Horse led me to the boardwalk and up the steps. I'd heard of rides and games somewhere out here, but Horse, like usual now, corrected me, told me I was thinking of Coney Island. He stopped at a bench, sat. The sun was mild, not that bright shit to make you put up your hands before you go fucking blind. Then Horse spoke:

—You know this is about to be it, I said, enough gravity in my voice that Ahab leaned left, pulled closer. A few hundred yards down, someone drove his truck onto the sand. A couple appeared. They started walking away. They didn't hold hands; she trailed after him but was in no hurry to catch up. Another couple, in the Jeep, were going at it. I turned to Ahab, said, I'm going to marry Melissa.

He nodded. —Sometimes I think everyone's fucking but me.

The way Ahab answered me, I understood what he thought I was into Melissa for, that in important ways, he didn't know me. The ocean was a terrible color but its noise was soothing. It made only one sound: the constancy of the shore coming back again and once more, always trying (maybe this time) to stay. You had to admire that kind of tenacity. I said, —How long was that contract you signed? Three years?

Ahab laughed and spat. —Yeah, you know, I'm just using those bitches for that paycheck. It don't mean nothing.

I shook my head. How could I explain it to him? All our lives I knew where we'd be hanging out, what girls were coming to a party. Despite the Marines or maybe because of, I was pretty sure all those stupid distractions of our childhood would keep Ahab happy for another six decades. Really, even joining the military was just his way to get anonymous sex and a regular paycheck for mindless work. Since last week at the recruiter's office, I'd been trying to convince him he could get both those silly goals fulfilled staying right where he was. Why add the slim chance you might lose your life? I asked often. Stay where you are. I said, —That sounds like a great way to live, for a paycheck.

I wanted to smack Horse. I was getting tired of sitting next to him, but then he unwrapped that old shirt and inside: a miniature of a giant warship—guns pointed forward, waiting to spit shells at the enemy, fuck up their towns.

He said, —For you, A, like when you're on board and that ship seems so huge, you can look at this and remember what the whole thing looks like. So it doesn't seem so immense. Horse passed it to me. The thing was heavy for the size. I tossed it from hand right to hand left.

Horse punched me in the arm. —It was this or buy you a copy of "In the Navy," but that might get you in trouble with your shipmates.

I watched him some more. The Marines had been filling my face with this talk of honor and power. Pride. It was swimming in my eyelids as I held this insult. Then I cocked my arm and gave one good toss. It almost reached the water. I said, —I'm in the fucking Marines. You even remember who I am?

Horse stood. —See, he said, now we have to go and get it. And he was right, of course. Even as it had been flying I knew I'd want it forever, a gift from my only true friend. Horse started walking to the steps.

We should have taken the stairs but Ahab was climbing the rails. To the top (there were three) and from there he, then me, plunked forward and down. Fifteen feet. When he landed he rolled into it like he'd already started practicing these things. Like he was having fantasies of bravery. When I landed I caught all those stinging kisses in my ankles. But one hop and we were on our feet, running quickly in the sand so greedy for our sneakers. Ahab and I reached the shore; there was the boat, beached; the sea came close, brushed against the bow. But our sudden movements hadn't put energy in Ahab alone, I was feeling something. I reached down and held the model, raised my arm and sent it out to the green, green water. When it landed it had gone so far you didn't even hear it splash. I looked at him and smiled with the challenge.

—That's how you want it? I asked Horse. In all our clothes, with the boardwalk watching, we ran into the sea. My legs were so strong I was jumping waves like fucking hurdles. The horizon didn't even seem that far, two big hops and we'd be there. Then the sea floor fell away and we were treading. Kept going, didn't stop until my lungs were thunder in my ribs.

I said, —Didn't think you'd keep up.

Horse laughed, but not happily. —Are you joking? We could keep going G.I. Joe. Right now. And all you could do is follow the trail of me kicking up water.

You would have thought Horse'd stopped sucking his thumb when he was ten, even twelve. Like normal motherfuckers. But when he was fifteen he was still doing it, in front of others, running his other hand over his ears, shutting his eyes. We had a plan so he would never need braces. Once a week, on his front steps, I'd lean my palms into his top teeth as hard as they could take; then I'd stop; he'd bite down on something, tell me about the pain in his fucking mouth, but that was a good sign, that they were shifted closer into place. We did it like that every week for years. When we were sixteen I was getting tired of his stupid plan and getting stronger, pushing hard even after he was tapping my elbow, then punching me.

—It's not so bad now, I said, laughing, after Ahab had reminded me of that scheme. I'd never tell him, but Melissa liked it when I whispered in her ear; the way my teeth bent in, the words came out with that little whistle and it tickled her ear. I did it every chance I got. She grabs my hand and squeezes it hard like she's angry, but when I look, man, she's always smiling. That stupid look on Ahab's face, I knew he couldn't understand anything more than what his crotch wanted. Dogs look like that, old ones: dumb.

Ahab asked, —Now how are we going to find that shit?

I said, —You've got better eyes than me, dip your head under. Like it was an order, Ahab went that fast. As though he'd been practicing obedience too. I admit, I watched him with contempt.

———

I dove in quick to get away from Horse. It was impossible to see, stupid to try. When my air ran out I went up, sucked deep and went in one more time. The second try, Horse grabbed the side of my head. Held me there. That was funny at first, true, but his arm was stiff and he gripped my hairs so tight I thought a few would come out. He was saying some shit, vibrations bounced around underwater, but I couldn't make it out. My eyes were burning. I tried to kick or push, but there was no leverage.

Horse pulled me back. I'd only been a foot under; my eyes went wide letting in that sunlight, so much it hurt, but I didn't have time to thank him as I inhaled. Inhaled. Now I could understand him, Horse was saying, —I'm leaving. I'm getting out. He was repeating this.

Eventually, I stopped. I floated there after Ahab came up. The far brown boardwalk, from the water, seemed like a fence put up around the farthest ends of this country. The way it ran in both directions I could believe it went three thousand miles, thirty. More. A perimeter. A guardrail. And who would be defending it? Ahab? This moron I'd grown up with? Who'd be at his post with nothing greater on his mind than the new rims he wanted on his car and in his hands a loaded gun? This was all funny, so I laughed at him.

Despite Horse's laughing, the attempt to drown me, I could ignore him. I was thinking of the uniform, how it would fit. With anticipation. For fucking days I had been watching television, thinking I had to pack in a lot of viewing time because when I went to boot camp I'd be spending all my hours doing sit-ups and marching in the rain. Four nights before, I came across this channel, the little gold H in the right bottom corner. All these white guys at desks, screaming. It was funny to me, this was almost forty years ago and they rocked electric blue blazers, thick-ass ties. It was when Nixon was going down, had done all that impeachable shit. Then the camera cuts to this one lady, behind a desk too; she's talking about her Country and her Constitution, which she loves. Loved. She spoke clearly, directly, all the ways Horse had been trying lately, hers had no sneer. Horse was an obnoxious motherfucker. I didn't tell him about Barbara Jordan. But watching her, how much she looked like me, it was the first time I'd thought my only options in the world weren't to be like Horse or to be like Sanford.

—Patriotism, Horse spat. A word he said all the time around me now. He said it like a curse.

—You know where patriotism is going to take you? I asked Ahab. To some brown country where you'll be told to shoot lots of brown people.

Ahab said, —You're still around when I'm on leave and I'll shoot you.

When I first mentioned I was leaving, changing neighborhoods and lives, I was all joyful. No parts regret. I enjoyed telling Ahab, slowly, which buses he could take to visit, knowing he never would. When I grabbed him tight in a hug, I know, it wasn't to show Ahab love. It was triumphant on my part, like in life I was the only hero. From how he was acting, Ahab might have been stupid enough to be feeling that way about America.

I left Horse behind, waited on the beach for maybe half an hour while he paddled out there, turning his back to the shore and staring at the far horizon, maybe thinking of his future like I was. When he finally came in we agreed the ship was lost, left like so many other things to drift on ocean currents for maybe five hundred years. On the bus we didn't speak. To be the fortunate son, even men like us wanted this.

In our neighborhood I walked to my house while Horse sped around the corner in a rush. He owned a Chevy, two-door, not sporty. It didn't run, two wheels were on cinder blocks, but he liked to sit in it like he might pull off. The radio worked. We lived barely a block apart, so when he got to it, I could hear the yelp of a rusted car door opening, the sound like bones being broken, loud like that.

two

one boy's beginnings

chuckie

So it was me, my boys and two new kids, Mark and Chuckie. All of us were heavy with equipment, the two new fellas with bikes. Saturdays parents existed only when we woke up and went to bed, the long line of hours in between were just baseball, baseball, baseball. We'd decided to stretch over to that park in the Italian neighborhood; the one near us was full.

The game went right: ground outs, pop flies and stolen bases; I slid into second after a line drive and caught a nice piece of glass in my knee, it left the kind of scar you could roll up your jeans and brag about. While waiting to swing a bat we made up stories about girls far off we were fingering. We were almost ten and spoke loudly.

Baseball diamonds had been etched into the park, three separate plots. It was easy to find little ponds all over; like everything in Flushing they looked good from a distance. Only coming closer could you spy their murky gray insides. In the summers, very faintly, they emitted paint fumes. It was getting dark. That's how night arrived then, bothering you all at once, bursting into the room. One of us said, —Let's get the fuck out of here. We weren't Italian. Not even Mark. Not even Chuckie. This is not to say I had no Italian friends, our neighborhood was a mash of origins, but still, there were intricate politics. This was 1982. You knew where you could be and when.

We gathered up our mitts and balls and both aluminum bats Jung had carried on his wide shoulders. Half a block traveled and I had to run back for the left-handed glove Mom bought special after searching through six different Modell's for a first baseman's. Then I chugged back to the guys on their feet, ahead of them Chuckie, Mark and the bikes they'd rode in on, these dope silver Huffys. Those two had learned how to do spins, other tricks, and instantly I hated them like I did all my boys: secretly. Those ties didn't mean much to me. When you stopped speaking to some kid there would be another; one thing Flushing had in abundance was people.

Ahead, Mark was screaming. For us. Chuckie too. We got closer quickly. Beyond them all the setting sun's flames were running down to an orange gasp on the horizon. Two sweaty boys gripped one set of handlebars each. They were old enough to buy beer. Smiling and Laughing, that might as well have been their names. One said, —Come on, let us ride them once.

Mark said, —I gotta get home, man. He sounded like he was going to cry.

—Me and my friend just want to ride around the corner, said the other one. Smiling.

—We gotta help them, Jung pleaded. He had invited them along so what else could he say? We weren't fifteen feet off. The two thieves hadn't noticed us, didn't look even as we crossed the street: moving away. Chuckie and Mark were on their own.

The trees all around had been season-stripped of every leaf; pulsing winds made the branches crash and shake like hands applauding. Mark turned to us, then Chuckie, they took a moment to stare. Only the arms of the older duo moved as they tugged and jerked the bikes. We heard yelling. The chain-link fence surrounding an old home swayed loosely, its rattle a language. —Guys, Jung tried again. We should really go over and help.

—Will you shut the fuck up, I said. I was afraid the

way people must be during a hurricane, thinking, Will
it come for me? I had seen fights, started and lost them,
I wasn't a novice. But this was a beating.

Mark was thrown off his bike. Next Chuckie. Then
the tall one was kicking Chuckie in the head. Mark got
up and ran—not toward us, just away. I couldn't tell
you how long those guys worked on Chuckie. It was a
few minutes. Even one or two are very long. The blood
started coming. I didn't know a face had so much.
Helping was still an option for the others, but not me;
it could have been Jung getting beat, my own father;
many people would call me the betrayer, often, but
that was because they'd mistaken me for a friend when
I was just hanging around. There was only one kid I
ever cared for and his name wasn't Chuckie. It wasn't
any of these guys.

When a loud -pop- echoed from across the street I
didn't flinch, wasn't even sure it had come from
nearby.

Ten is too young to learn how you are. That you
wouldn't run for the ambulance, as all my friends did,
while Chuckie clutched at his eye like his very own
soul was in danger of escaping. Booth Memorial didn't
send an ambulance quickly. To the right, in the park,
squirrels appeared, ruthlessly picking at the ground for
food; from where I stood their quick little hops were
even more graceful; when they ate energetically they
seemed to be on their knees, paws forward in a frantic
prayer.

Trinidad

I

Of the four of us I was the yellow one, getting closer and closer to brown; sunlight burned down so hot I wasn't sure if it was a punishment or a blessing.

Vaughn was a coolie and that red-brown skin of his matched his bright new bike; the one saying, My mummy has money, every time a wind blew and sent the rainbow-colored tassels on his handlebars flying. Orpheus had called it a bitchy bike when we'd first witnessed it, but what he'd meant to say was, I wish it was mine. Those two were the same age as me; our last member was Orpheus's little brother, Caesar, who rode far back, two years behind us; he was eight. Caesar pumped his skinny little legs harder to catch up, as though he could pedal his way to our maturity.

My bike was new too, but not as fancy. Back in New York I would have beat up kids who rode things as nice as what I now had. Me and my boys would have kicked his ass twice. But in Trinidad it wasn't like that. It wasn't about my mother the secretary who couldn't afford much. Here it was Aunty Barbara who paid; she had all that loot from the dead doctor, a husband who had insured that money would never be the problem. Orpheus and Caesar had bikes like the one leaning behind my couch in Flushing, Queens. Their mother, Lucille, cleaned house for my Aunty, Vaughn's mom and others. The four of us had met on Aunty Barbara's front porch, an evening planned by three kinds of mothers: by birth—Orpheus and Caesar; by law— Vaughn was adopted; and by substitution—that would be mine.

We stopped pedaling when Orpheus complained that his seat was loose. I flopped down in grass beside the dirt road that would lead to the fulfillment of a promise: the best homemade curry goat on the island. Lucille was going to do the cooking. I was anticipatory. —Fix it quick.

—Shut up New York, Orpheus said, both hands on

the bike seat, working his weight down. We watched as it sank some, but not enough.

Vaughn's mother spent money and expected things to last. She hadn't married a doctor but became one; there were only about ten black women in Trinidad who could say this. Vaughn had to bring his bike home dirt-free and shiny-shiny; even grass trapped in the chain could get him in trouble. His bike stood like it was still in a shop window between mine and Caesar's, the ones flat on their sides.

We three, on our backs, looked at the sky, thinking our privacies.

Orpheus said, —I'm ready. But no moves were made, doing nothing felt too good. I had known only New York sun my whole life, the one spectacular in the way it erases winter, but I had hardly ever had grass and dirt beneath me, air empty of a million other people's breaths. The grass rubbed at my back, coarse and half dead from all that light and no rain. Bugs landed on our motionless knees and explored. They attacked the skin, but their bites were still gentler than what I was used to.

II

Me and Malik had been tight for years. But I had never met his father until that Saturday. Malik and I were

nine, lived at the same address. When he'd asked,
—You want to meet my father? I'd said, —Sure.

In the lobby, going from my side of the building to
his, we passed the old women who got together in
groups to cackle. If it was warmer they'd have been on
the sidewalk in their lawn chairs. When me and Malik
walked through that afternoon they had been there for
hours. They wore loose house dresses and, most often,
slippers. They pulled back their lips as we passed,
ready to talk more shit as soon as we were gone. The
long wall to our right had this huge picture of a sunrise,
but it never made warmth. In the elevator I asked
Malik, —Where's your dad been?

—I don't know. He showed up.

I nodded. I hadn't seen my father my whole life.
When I saw some white dude I resembled coming
down the block I would ask my mother, —Is that him?
She would laugh and say, —Do you see my black ass
running? No, she wouldn't have said the curse, but it
was there in the intonation.

At the door to his apartment Malik turned to me.
—Call him Mr. Stewart.

—Is that your last name? He looked at me like I
wasn't serious, but I was.

Their apartment was like mine: living room,
kitchen, bathroom, one bedroom he shared with his
mother like I did mine. There was a second bedroom,
but his was always locked; in my apartment, D23,

my grandmother slept there, all on her own like a queen. Malik's place was always dark, his moms had sensitive eyes, a medical condition, kept the curtains drawn. There were safety pins running up them like a stitch. I thought I was in the wrong place for a second because it was full of light. His father sat on the couch. This man said, —Your mother's taking a nap.

—Okay.

—Who's this?

—Anthony, I said. Hello, Mr. Stewart.

We shook. —I like that. Malik, go find me some beer.

Malik nodded and disappeared. —Sit down. Mr. Stewart motioned to the couch with his chin. So how old are you?

—Nine.

—Same age as Malik?

—Uh-huh. I wished the television was on, just for the distraction. Mr. Stewart stared at me. We stayed like this. I was curious about him, he seemed strange. Mr. Stewart had pulled open the curtains, the remnants of safety pins lay on the carpet, mangled. Malik returned with a beer.

—Hey, Mr. Stewart shouted after some gulps. I know where I've seen you before. At the Key Food. Was that your mom I saw you with? Black lady? My age?

—Yes.

—Boy, your mom sure is nice looking. He grinned. You know what I'm talking about Malik?

Malik looked at his father like he was speaking Slavic dialect. —What?

—Awww, his father shrugged, you boys can't see gold because you're too busy looking for bubble gum.

Again Malik was mystified. Me too.

—Never mind, Mr. Stewart sighed, shrugged, finished the beer. He reached into his pants, pulled out a five. You and Anthony take this and go out for a while, I'm going to wake your mother. He ushered us on, Take your time. I hear kids out there. Have fun. Couple of hours.

Malik and I were out the door. I'd spied the bill as Malik had been stuffing it into the pocket of his Kangaroos. —Thank you, I yelled at the door. Your dad is great, I said in a lower voice. I was serious. Enthusiastic.

Malik nodded, walked. —He's going to be here for about a week, so we could probably get a bunch more money out of him.

When the elevator arrived I held it while Malik went to the stairs for a piss. Five floors down people screamed up the shaft, —Let go of the goddamn button! I didn't. When we reached the lobby we rushed through the crowd of adults trying to tell us manners. Outside, we passed kids leaning against Mr. Russin's Chevy. We walked for a candy store. Malik put his arm around my shoulders.

III

It became a race for the four of us as we neared Lucille's home. Caesar was in last place, ready to cry or at least curse, and right near him Vaughn, going slow and eyeing the dirt cautiously for rocks, a dent that might send him flying. Me and Orpheus, though, we were moving.

We had been pedaling through countryside; soon we'd reach where houses had been built up cheaply and in close ranks. Before I saw their brick bodies, tin roofs, I heard the sounds of animals living all over the place.
—What's that fucking noise? I screamed.

Orpheus laughed loud enough for me to hear. —That's goat, New York, you been living in the city too long.

The road curved. The air should have smelled like something sweeter but there was only the hard odor of burning tires. It should have been a problem, but there was so much space here, all that sky above, that you couldn't imagine the scent would choke you forever; winds would come along eventually to usher the stench of charred rubber out to the ocean and after it would come something else, perhaps as pleasant as mangoes. We passed the old woman with a machete who liked to swing it near kids who made her vexed. We were ten feet farther before she had lifted that steel sword. Only Caesar yelped with fear as he weaved away.

Lucille stood in front of her home sucking on a Marlboro. She smiled as we came to a quick stop, skidding, spraying dirt with our tires. She put her hand over her lit cigarette until the little cloud settled. She hugged her son, then me. —Hi Miss Cooper, I said.

She touched my face, her hands smelled like car oil. —I told you to call me Aunty Lucille.

The fence guarding their house was old wire. A dog was passed out from the heat, lying in the road. The tongue was slung out the right side of its mouth; the animal could barely manage a pant. I went over and knelt down, put my hand on its side. I was all sympathy. Aunty Lucille was at me quick, pulling me back by my hair. —Boy! Are you stupid?

I looked at her with my urban incredulity. —It wasn't going to bite me.

She laughed. Orpheus laughed. Caesar. Even Vaughn.

—What's funny? What's funny? I looked at the dog, which had twisted its head enough for one half-open eye to gaze at me. The dog's fur was the muddy yellow of every mutt I've ever seen—me included.

—Don't you never get around animals, New York? Orpheus took me in with amazement.

—I see pigeons.

Caesar stood beside me while I lifted my bike. He said, —You're going to have to wash your hands a lot before we eat. I looked at him with a question. The dog, man, he said, exasperated. Too dirty for touch.

Yards were filled: with old cars, older cars, wrecked cars, a truck, bikes, shovels, cinder blocks, fallen trees, sheets of tin, strips of wood, bent metal, street signs, a wheelbarrow full of rocks, propane, gasoline, porcelain figurines of a very white Jesus, porcelain figurines of a very black Jesus, many tires as yet uncooked.

Aunty Lucille walked away from us, to one of her girlfriends. Orpheus kicked away his sneakers and I followed after he'd told me I wouldn't be served goat wearing tennis shoes; he hated that I never took them off.

Orpheus took me around the back of the house. Bugs attacked my fresh feet. Every three steps I had to knock away some gorged winged insect from a toe. I submitted my feet to the sun. We came to a tree, thicker and taller than the one in front; tied to it were three goats making their noises. I jumped back like: ready to run. —It's just goats! Orpheus yelled. And they're tied up.

The rope binding them was dense and awful; in places it had been chewed. It was very strong stuff and those goats would never bite through in time. They smelled, their faces reminded me of Evil Professors; their gray eyes, lids half shut, convinced me they were planning things. —Can I pet them? I asked.

—What's wrong with you? City boy always wants to pet things and play with them. These things are for eating.

The goats were their own beings. One of them was

an asshole. It shuffled a hoof in the dirt and knocked a pebble at me. Orpheus walked off shaking his head, but I stayed, hypnotized by this foe. The other two ignored me, but this one peeled back its face and gave me the show—the dentals were uneven and sharp. Then it wailed out at me. The sound was stiff and angry, bad and bad.

—Shut up, I told it.

It repeated the noise. I walked closer and it moved forward. The fur was gray. Again, the noise. The fur was matted down. I got closer, maybe if it was played with it wouldn't do that. It wasn't the normal sound of goats; the others used their throats in the usual way. Tones I didn't love, but I could bear. This goat was on some other shit.

I thought of putting my hand on the thing, but its whole body seemed ready for a fight. Not a big animal, still its tight form looked like it could generate some power. I tilted my head and one watched the Other. Aunty Lucille called for me, telling me to wash my hands. Some chickens in the next yard started their clucking. The chorus was alarming. Confusing. Every animal sounded ugly. Then the goat came down on my naked toes with one of those motherfucking hooves.

A twenty-five-pound weight had been dropped purposely on my foot once and it had felt better than this. The hoof rifled down at me quick, then the goat was off with its friends. I was on my back, clinging to my toes.

I yelled and Aunty Lucille appeared with ice. Blood spilled over the cubes as she rubbed them on the busted skin. I curled my toes and the pain was worse. The blood rivered down my elevated foot, to my ankle, my shin. My friends had been inside watching television, but came out to survey the damage done. Even Vaughn, who never admitted it, was impressed.

I thought to myself, this isn't so bad. In a month this goat had been my only attacker. The other twenty-nine days had been solid peace and safety. This isn't so bad, I reassured myself again, in the kitchen, as Aunty Lucille cut greens and told me jokes. I sipped a cup of Milo, my foot was up on a chair. When it came time for the meat I asked Aunty Lucille if I could pick the goat.

IV

Malik and me with five dollars to spend was a wonderful, wonderful thing. Malik revealed that Lincoln occasionally on the way to the store; I was young enough to believe that it alone was the source of a certain freedom. That five hundred pennies made us affluent.

I told him, —At Manaro's they got Now & Laters for cheap.

He had almost no eyebrows. He frowned often. He asked, —What the fuck you want to go out there for?

—I just told you. Now & Laters. Cheap.

Malik waited on the corner. Down the block was GinaRose, where candy was higher priced but safe to buy. Six blocks to Manaro's. I could convince that kid to do anything if I smiled enough. I was persuasive.

The Italian kids ran blocks as well as the rest of us. Manaro's was theirs; a place that sold candy, magazines, deli food and drinks, most neighborhoods have a few. But in Flushing everything was tightly packed so that from the air you'd think integration, but down at sidewalk level, segregated was the rule. No one complained about borders except when they were crossed. That shit was suicide.

So me and Malik were suicidal over candy.

We passed the little businesses: pastry shops and liquor stores. Old women paced the blocks in groups of two to four, staring at us in simple amazement because everyone knew the general rules. By the time we reached Manaro's we were moving at a slow jog.

Inside, old men were talking in their various native tongues; only the trained ear could detect the momentary pause and assessment when Malik and I entered. We proceeded to fill our hands. The man behind the counter counted what we gave him, told us a price. I put some of the candy in my pockets. Malik knew the routine: put the five in the man's hand, forget reciprocal courtesy and pick up the change dropped on the countertop. This shit had been the practice since my Aunty Pecola was a girl. The store smelled of the eggplants being cooked in the back. The gathered men talked louder and we were reminded, in this way, to go.

We were out man, ghost.

Everything would have been fine, we'd have been back on our street laughing at how simple it had been if they hadn't opened a comic-book shop.

—Fuck.

Who said it first? I don't know, but there we were, pressed to the front window, chins against the light splotches of dirt that had not been washed away. Malik had three dollars left. His face, reflected in the glass, was as happy as mine. The kind behind us were less cheerful.

I turned. Malik turned. One of these boys started talking shit. I knew him. From school. We were better friends there than on the street, most of us were. This kid had very short arms, a face like the back of a fridge; he did book reports that made teachers cry—with illustrations and legible handwriting. Danny.

We got running.

We ran.

Fast.

Them catching me was the sensation where you feel the pain before it gets there. These kids who were all boredom or brainlessness had me around the neck, on my legs. They led me and Malik down the streets like we were trophies. We passed the GreenPoint Savings Bank where my mother often did transactions. When with her, I was safe; adults were your traveling papers, signed, the only way you were going to fly out of Casablanca.

As we came to Flushing Meadows Park it seemed, in my limited vision, that their numbers had doubled. I had been trying to escape, but the kid with his limb around my throat only held tighter when I moved. More when I screamed. It was the same for my boy, so eventually we lay in their arms limp and silent.

You could look forward to a specialized torment depending on who got their hands on you. If you were on our block, the Universal Beatdown was the practice: seven-on-one, thirteen-on-three; fair fights had gone out of style in '78, when I was six. By '82 we had all developed, grown. And these kids, the Italians, had the pole.

It wasn't a specific one, any basketball court had the proper equipment. Some silver twelve-foot monster. This bunch was talking but I was not eavesdropping. I was hearing only me and my concerns: those Now & Laters spilling from my pockets, their light taps on the concrete almost lost in all the footsteps.

So we got the poling. The whole thing: legs spread, a guy at either foot, pulling; another boy lifting your shoulders, pushing; the pole and nuts connecting. The pain. The screaming. The more pain as pole and balls were reintroduced. The crying.

They left.

On my back the world above seemed infinite. I lay

there understanding how I might exist as an eight-inch man: the planet would not be big, it would be colossal; there would be no exploration of the outer atmospheres, the tops of trees might suffice. From here I could see out of the park, to the intersection nearby—to the arm of that pole reaching out over the road and at its tip the traffic light shining like a terrific gold medallion.

My face was under tears; I managed to roll left, see Malik, who was similar. His eyes were closed. My dick was so full of heat I thought it might be bleeding. The throbbing attacked my stomach, the tops of my legs. I tried to explain this to Malik for some reason, but couldn't find any words. I had lost my breath.

This was the give and take of all our ethnic wars. We were the future janitors and supermarket managers, plumber's assistants and deliverymen of the United States. Flushing is not like this anymore. A civilization has been lost. Minor Herodotus I will be, in remembering it all; our lives, to me, are important artifacts.

My mother walked in on us rubbing each other on my tenth birthday. I was supposed to see a movie with my uncle. There was no party because it was a weekday. To her it must have looked like Malik and I were dancing, his back against the wall. We weren't touching, not most of us. That's what it was like.

When the door opened I didn't hear it. The sound the

carpet made brushing up against the door bottom didn't warn me of anything. There had never been a lock, but when my mother pulled at my arm I fell onto my bed, thinking, How did she get in here? Malik stood against the wall with his eyes closed and his lip bit. Like silent movie reels, scenes skipped by: my mother putting her arm around Malik's neck, my mother and Malik leaving the bedroom, me following them; my mother slamming the front door and locking it, pushing me into the bedroom and pulling the door closed from the outside. —Stay in there, she said woodenly through the wall; I crawled backward, wrapping my sheets around me.

I didn't realize I had fallen asleep until Uncle Isaac was shaking me awake.

He sat on the edge of my bed with his back to me. He turned and looked over his shoulder. —Your mother tells me something happened today.

I stared at his short afro my mom said all jobs found acceptable. He moved like he was going to face me but then he wouldn't. I wished I had heat vision so I could burn a hole through his skull and all the things he'd been told could leak out onto my bedspread. Then I could soak it all up and throw the cover out the window, out of our lives forever and he wouldn't have to look at me the way he did when he finally turned around. —Instead of a movie, he said, let's go play some basketball.

I nodded, tied sneakers in silence; he watched me.

Outside, my uncle bounced the ball like a pro. He wore his loafers, slacks, a button-down shirt, but he moved like a kid.

—Anthony!

My friends were climbing the parking lot fence across the street. It was the place kids could go to do football or stickball without having to stop every time a car came crawling down the block. I waved. They forgot about me as they disappeared over the chain-link. I looked up at my uncle, thought of asking him if I could go with them, but I was afraid of this motherfucker when he was in a good mood. It seemed like the same fat garbage floated before all the apartment buildings; in snowy winters when the mounds were covered in white, we'd scale them like tiny Matterhorns. I waved away some flies.

—Come on, Uncle Isaac called to me as he stood at the mouth of the park.

People were coming and going, it was chilly. The older ones sat on the benches that circled the park, all concrete and not any grass, talking to one another out of the sides of their faces and wiping their necks. We passed the small brick building that once had open bathrooms, when I was seven. The only thing that worked now was the water fountain. My man Dennis was holding his little sister up so she could get a good mouthful. I waved at him; he nodded.

Near the handball walls one tired-ass rim hung limply, begging for someone to notice. I clutched my balls at the sight of another pole. We stood at the thing, Uncle Isaac stretched his legs. —You should warm up, he said. You'll hurt yourself.

I moved in different directions, but my body felt so closed up I was surprised I could lift my hands above my head. He passed me the rock. —Shoot it. Let's see what you've got. I held the ball like it was a punchline.

—Shoot the goddamn thing.

I threw it, watched it sail over the other side of the backboard. Sounded like thunder when it landed on the ground, echoing among the buildings that surrounded the park on all sides. —That's okay, Uncle Isaac said. He ran the ball down and threw it back at me. I shot again, missed. Run it down, he insisted. I walked it back. He put out his hands, I tossed it to him. He dribbled at the free-throw line, rocked back and forth, stared at the basket like he was in the Final Four. Anthony, he said. What happened today, with your friend. With Malik. It can't happen.

I couldn't lift my head for anything; I stared at his shoes, the toes a little nicked.

—Did you hear me?

—Yes, I said.

—Well?

—It won't happen again. I started to cry.

He stopped bouncing the ball. Watched me. —Turn those off.

I wiped my eyes and sucked it in.

—Now this kid Malik, I think you should keep away from him.

—He's my best friend!

—Well, you know what he's going to become?

I didn't answer.

—He's going to turn out funny.

—Funny?

—You know. A faggot.

—Oh, I said.

He bounced the ball a little easier. —And do you know what faggots do?

—I don't want to know, I said. Can we go home Uncle Isaac?

—Faggots put their dicks in each other's mouths.

I made a face. Then I said, —What?

—That's right. Is that what you want?

I knew the answer to that one, fuck no. —No.

—Good.

He took me to Baskin-Robbins, where he let me put two scoops on a cone. He was still a little worried so he mentioned this island, Trinidad. I listened as we walked by apartment buildings. If I was remembering right, we passed the one where four girls had hurled glass bottles at us as we stood in their courtyard. When Uncle Isaac was through, he'd explained that they didn't want to send me away, but would if I kept acting wrong. I was sold.

So I planned it. Both our families watched us closer. But one afternoon Mom and Grandma had gone to the doctor and I convinced Malik to come use my Atari. We played *Dodge 'Em* furiously because it was the only game that worked. I'd taken the others apart to learn of the brittle mechanism inside, had expected more than a wafer-thin board of green and silver. I kept going to the living room, spying out the window until I saw the two ladies returning. Then, back in my room, I pawed at Malik. He had a small head shaped like a cashew nut; he was good looking and we loved each other the way boys often do. He hesitated, said that his father would be taking him to Chicago if we were caught again, that he should be going. I thought of Trinidad and how it wasn't Flushing. Malik was my truest friend. I smiled. And I persuaded, showed him I was willing to go further than before. When I heard the keys at the door I coughed loudly so Malik wouldn't be warned. This time, when they found us, we were in our underwear.

V

My mother came to get me.

My mother with a vacation, off from typing letters

and filing things. End of August and here she was: the dress was new and Aunty Barbara was complimentary.

—Thank you, my mother said. Sitting in the living room Mom sipped tea like she was a part of Aunty's set: the pinky out, the ankles together as well as the knees. It was afternoon, my bags were packed, the new bike had been given to Orpheus. I walked outside and onto the front porch. Down to the black gate, its paint dried over little clumps of dirt, I rubbed those raised bumps against the back of my hand.

My mother came out with laughing Barbara, both walked down the stairs. Aunty turned to me, her appropriate gold earrings framing her stern face. She smiled and threw open her arms. —Come give your Aunty a hug. I grabbed around her middle as she laughed and held me tight. Her earring, sharp at the corners, was cutting into the side of my face. I wasn't going to move until she let go; I liked the way she felt when she laughed.

My mother admired the plants.

—Are we going now? I asked Mom.

—No, but soon.

—Can we see a movie? I asked.

She took me, after dinner and in Aunty's car. Driving it, there was a pleasure on my mother's face I hadn't seen before. It was that face that enjoys ownership, even temporarily.

My mother chose the flick; I bought the candy and

giant soda. She paid for everything. The theater was a place that should have been for royalty—giant ceilings, carpets everywhere, all the things. We climbed two sets of stairs, weighed down with food. At dinner my mother had put her hands on my face as though she wanted something from me.

—What's wrong? I asked as we found two good seats.

—You really going to eat all this? she asked, pointed.

I nodded. —Of course. This is nothing.

The lights died and the screen -blip-, -blip-, -blipped- to life. Projector noise filtered down to us. On with the film: the first one was easy, some violence, more violence—a guy taking the streets back from the vermin (human). I got through it fine; my mother was quiet, covered her eyes when people were being shot and when an old lady had her finger pliered off by some kid in a mask.

This wasn't a popular place so to get any money they had to do a double feature. The second was as bad as the first, this one had a lady with a giant chest. She was a spy and a martial artist; she got in fights over and over. Ten seconds into every melee something tore her shirt off—a knife, someone's hand, a strong wind. Any chance for this woman to pop out a tit. I was enthralled.

But you know how it is, I was watching this shit with my mother.

I was rocking a hard-on like you wouldn't believe—I

was impressed anyway. But I couldn't sit back and let it go, next door was the lady who'd cleaned my ass once. I was leaning forward so my waist wasn't exposed, but the thing kept groaning against my little shorts; it was so persistent I thought it was making noise. By about the third breast explosion I stopped thinking about my dick and looked at my mother, offered her some candy. The lady was in tears. I mean the big stuff, the ugly stuff. —Mom, what's wrong?

She touched my head, grimaced. —Don't you think she's pretty? Mom motioned, the screen. Do you?

I was lost. —What?

—Well, you're just sitting there. Like it's nothing.

I shook my head, laughed at what she didn't know; funny wasn't how she was feeling.

—You have to stop, Anthony. You have to stop being like this.

—What are you talking about? I leaned into her weeping face.

—You can't live this way. You don't want to do this. I don't know why you would do this to me. To you. Stop it. It'll be bad.

But they were silly tears and I had the erection to prove it. I wanted to thank her. She'd thought that sending me here was a punishment, as though I were banished. I never wanted to go back to Flushing.

—I want to hear you promise me, she said. Promise you won't be Malik's friend anymore.

Each night, going to bed, I remembered why I hated home, the response that had been trained into me: expect the awful, revel in it. In Trinidad I was another boy, not so quick to be venal and petty. I cared some. But when my mother arrived the reality that I would have to return was exhausting, made me panic. In the theater I tried to think how I might stay longer, even a day, an hour. If she was content here, felt at ease, I thought she might relax into this island, quit her job and stay. Here, she wouldn't be the woman who'd ask a ten-year-old for such a pledge. I hadn't asked about Malik those three summer months. I never mentioned his name. I didn't want to return and find out, though I missed him enough that I could cry. I thought, How can I make this woman happy? —That's not too hard, I told her.

—You don't think so? she asked, so much hope in her voice, dying to be convinced.

I told her, —It's nothing. I conceded, Malik is just a faggot anyway.

who we did worship

Olisa said she loved me and she'd eat glue to prove it. In sixth grade she went around saying she wanted a boy who was like her and that left only me and this African kid, we called him Ojigatoo but that wasn't his name. So really, in our school, that left me because the only thing anyone did with Ojigatoo was chase him, throw rocks and call him an African Bootie Scratcher. And when I say anyone, I mean everyone.

Me and her weren't friends. In school or out. With her short afro like mine, she came up to me in the schoolyard, told me and the world how she felt. They all heard, from the wall where boys played handball to the fence where girls jumped rope.

—What? I asked again, surprised.

She repeated herself. —I said, I love you.

—Who the fuck are you? I screamed, more for the crowd. I didn't want to admit I'd ever seen her, knew her name.

Other kids laughed. Someone called out, —That's one ugly bitch, and I thought, she sure is. I'm not talking plain, but the kind of ugly where you wanted to slap her parents for having fucked. She smiled like I should be happy too. I thought that if an ugly girl liked me that meant I looked as bad as she did, that ugly people stuck together like the middle class.

—Leave me alone, I said. Probably it sounded a bit like begging.

—No. Single-family homes surrounded our school; they had porches bordered by wobbly iron railing painted white, black or green. I expected people to come out and gaze at us from there, a show for the world. So I did what an eleven-year-old boy does, I ran.

She came after me. She was slower, so the farther I got the louder she screamed my name, —Anthony! Anthony!

Even the older women who played monitor during lunch and in the mornings came to see us running around, a traveling coon show right in their town. Ojigatoo was perched in his lonely corner, laughing. I wanted to stop long enough to throw a rock at his ass, remind him of the hierarchies and his awful position within them. Finally she couldn't run anymore. I passed near the sidewalk outside our gated schoolyard, my reflection revealed in a car window. My expression.

Some little kid gets me thinking about Olisa. The memory comes as easy as a cookie with your tea. In a pizza parlor, me inside the bathroom, his seven- or eight-year-old hand twisting the doorknob on the other side. I shook my dick off, called to him, —I'll be done in a second. Stepped out, rubbing my hands on my jeans because there were no paper towels by the sink. I looked down at the boy's face: beautiful, brown like mine; his eyes grew wide as he moved backward, could have broken into a run in an instant, to his father who was placing a little green jacket on the back of a chair. A pair of red gloves hung from the sleeves, connected to each other by a red string that ran inside the arms and across the back so he would never lose them. —I don't need to use that bathroom anymore, Papa.

The father was surprised, tired and angry. He looked up to find me staring, the object of his son's disaffection. The kid snaked himself between his father's legs, looked like he would have crawled right up his dad's asshole if he could. Anything to get farther from me. —Kids, the father muttered to me. He was trying to play it off and I appreciated the act. He had a mustache and a beard going gray in small amounts. His hands were thick, he gripped his chair tight, then released. He and his son wore an expression I'd seen before.

I pictured this man writing a letter to his family back in Puerto Rico or the Dominican Republic, telling them how cold it gets in February here in New York City, not thinking to mention how crazy the boy acted one afternoon getting pizza when confronted with some kokolo who could have easily been a cousin. Why explain to them what they already knew? The father wiped his expression away because by that age you know how, but his son was unable to hide and I thought of me and Olisa. And Nancy, her too.

Now you want to talk about beautiful?

Then you had to discuss Nancy Salvino. There was no one prettier in school. Loved by every boy from first grade to sixth. I would watch her on my own; sometimes fellas got together to stare.

—I would fuck the shit out of her, Mark said, fingering that messed-up tooth of his, the one that bent in slightly and had gone brown. It had happened after a very bad fall; he'd run away from a beating, so fast he lost his footing close to his home.

Sanjay, who hardly hung around us, stood there rapt, said, —She's so pretty. I wish she were my girlfriend.

I stopped, pointed and announced sincerely, —You are one big fag.

Not just for that statement did I call him that, also he was a milk monitor once a week, stationed at the end of the lunch line by the big refrigerated metal milk mausoleum. He took it serious. He wore a mustard yellow vest over his button-down shirts every day. He wore slacks. After he'd handed out all the milk, he had to wipe down the insides of the apparatus with a rag; he'd lean into corners and conscientiously scrub. When he did we'd run up on him, push him inside, pull down the top and shove a pen in the space meant for a lock. He would be inside yelling, banging, while we kicked the sides of the box, screaming, —Sanjay! You fucking Hindu!

Later, after his release, he'd come to us, explaining, —You know, I'm not a Hindu. Hinduism is a religion.

Our standard response to all intelligent assertions was a barrage of punches in the shoulder or chest.

In class we learned of the Untouchables—lowest caste in India. Miss Bernstein showed us slides: images of people bathing in a river and wonderful countrysides, a whole family of blue-black Untouchables standing before a tiny hut. Kids laughed at that sight, but I stared at the old man smiling wide and looking like my grandfather.

After that lesson, we would chase Sanjay on the days we weren't friends, screaming after him that he too was an Untouchable, laughing as we said it. When we did this I'd imagine Sanjay in the bathroom, at his mirror, running hands across his skin, wondering why he was dull brown and not a lighter shade. I thought, Why should I be the only one asking myself that question? Sanjay did not hang out with us too much.

After her announcement, the days with Olisa were awful. She wouldn't stop, reminded me incessantly of what I had not at all forgotten. I expected a break only in Gym, when we had to change and guys swarmed into the locker room. In there I thought I was free of her, but then One-Eyed Chuckie asked, —So, Anthony. You got a girlfriend?

—Shut up, you fucking cyclops, I said. Everyone laughed; One-Eyed Chuckie, who was sensitive about it, slammed his locker shut and left.

—Seriously, Ant, Mark said while sliding on shorts. You going to go out with Olisa?

I was shocked, angry at the suggestion. —No fucking way. I looked down, my face warm. She's so ugly.

—Yeah, someone added. You see that hair? Does she comb that shit or what?

I sat and pulled on my sneakers. Mark asked me, —How does she get her hair like that?

—How would I know? I hopped up like we might fight.

—Okay. Don't get mad. Mark tapped me on the arm. She is fucking ugly though, he said as though that was an apology.

We walked out to the yard. Kids were choosing up

sides for kickball. The maroon ball lay on the gray, pebbled yard waiting for someone to direct some energy toward it. The sun was well above the fence line and its glow felt like a pressure against my forehead, not heat, something physical. —It's kind of windy, I said.

—Okay, Mark agreed.

—I better go get my hat, I said and ran inside.

But about Nancy.

I was watching her on my own as she stood, with Miss Bernstein, going over a spelling test. Nancy was into that Madonna look back then, as much as she could afford—the layers of cut-up clothing. She was close too, her brown hair framed her face well; it was all a mass of strategically messy curls. Nancy wasn't allowed to wear makeup yet.

Mostly, watching her, I wanted sex. In my head a whisper asked, What if she did let you fuck her? What if she said yes and showed you her pussy? I had seen only magazines by this point, porno movies were a year away; in the snapshots I'd pawed, the way women had to hold themselves open made me think there was a complicated system of flaps to undo before you got inside. I was afraid that when I was finally close to one I'd have to sit back and ask the girl to work the shit for me.

Todd, droopy ears and big teeth, saw me staring, came and said, —I dare you to grab her ass. He didn't say it quiet so other guys left what they were breaking to swarm around me like I was giving away quarters for video games. For twenty minutes, in the afternoons, Miss Bernstein gave us free time and Todd's challenge was indicative of how well we used the period.

—Go ahead, look at her ass in those jeans.

—Man, you should just go and sink your teeth into it.

—Just go over there and fuck her in the ass! Rich joked; someone smacked him for the rest of us—serious plans were being made.

—I'll do it.

Guys laughed.

—Yeah, bullshit.

—You won't do it you faggot.

I stood. I walked at her. The chairs behind me scraped the green floor as my friends arranged themselves into an auditorium audience, row after row. Why couldn't Miss Bernstein walk away?

Next to them now, Miss Bernstein smiled pleasantly. I was a good student. Twice she had hugged my mother after parent-teacher nights. Nancy did not turn her head to me. Her ass however, spoke: Go ahead, it goaded. What's the big whoop? My hand began its trajectory and I cheered it on. Started low and I envisioned a perfect cup of the right or left cheek, but then my five fingers had their own plan, wanted something else. Up her back, close but not touching, to the shoulder, over the other side and finally the motherfucker perched there on Nancy Salvino's left breast.

I was scared to move or squeeze. Miss Bernstein's eyes darted from my hand to my face. Her grill lit up like magnesium flares. I was smiling, then, fuck it, I squeezed.

Miss Bernstein stuttered out, —What the shit are you doing? The laughs, behind me, were an explosion—so powerful I would have ducked if I wasn't hypnotized. Girls stopped writing their friends' names on the covers of their notebooks. Nancy turned, looked at me, didn't seem angry. We asked so much of that girl, like she was the God of All Our Needs. She looked at me like I was stupid, like I could be sure this was the closest I'd ever get.

Miss Bernstein yelled as she led me from the class. She was tall and had long, frizzy brown hair that she often wore up; she was in her forties and none of us had ever had a crush on her. She squeezed my hand too tight as we moved; instantly I got an erection. The way her wedding ring rubbed against my wrist bone, she was really trying to hurt me.

In his office Principal Kurdick talked to me so slow and precise that I got drowsy. He said, —I can tell you feel awful. I looked around the room for whoever he was addressing. You can go back to your class now, he said. Miss Bernstein watched him, waiting for more; when nothing came we went together, she angrier at the principal now than me. She told me, in case I hadn't understood, what I'd done wrong. As we moved my hand throbbed with power, heat and majesty that would have been called bragging if my mouth were doing it.

After school me, Frankie, Jung and Mark walked home. We stopped at the Carvel across the street from Booth Memorial Hospital, which had a horror story attached to it, a caution for all children who might hurt themselves. Its ambulances were slow.

—You're stupid, Frankie said to me as he licked the chocolate ice cream dripping down his hand. The walk home was nice; gas stations across the street leaked so much intoxicating fumes there was no way you couldn't inhale a bunch.

I assured him, —Metallica is much better than Iron fucking Maiden. I was eating a strawberry Flying Saucer. I took a bite.

Jung shook his head. —Judas Priest. Fucking Judas Priest.

—What do you know? I laughed. He gave me a shot in the shoulder, it hurt, but I smiled. You punch like a girl.

—Faggot, Mark added absently.

The four of us walked on, debating in this manner, passing the black gates of the Botanical Gardens. We reached Tony's building, his was like most: dim hallways and piss on the stairs. Mark lived in a rented home with his mother and two brothers; they'd had me over one weekend and taken me to their synagogue. Frankie lived with his dad somewhere farther. I'd see his father around in his old clothes, a fading denim jacket, looking impotent and angry about it, the world already poised to forget him and his hard work.

We rang the bell five times before Tony got to the door, sweating. He was out of breath, stooped forward with his elbows on his knees. Jung asked, —You jerked off so much you got tired?

—My mom's birds got out, Tony said.

Jung leaned back against a wall, we were all inside, said something in Korean; Tony nodded, sadness on his face. I nodded for him too, understood, Your mom is going to kill you, in Korean, Urdu, Pakistani, Spanish and Italian.

—Take off your shoes, Tony commanded.

Mark laughed. —This ain't Japan. Me and Frankie went to the living room couch, my sneakers and his boots cutting like knives across the carpet. Tony still looked worried.

—Why don't we catch them? I asked.

Frankie went to the kitchen and returned with five garbage bags. —We each take one and hunt these fucks down.

All armed, we moved together, through the living room. We passed the television (on), the bookshelf, the couches, the small table where new mail was dropped.

There was birdseed, small pebbles of it, lying on surfaces. Tony explained that he'd tried to lure them with it, get them to stop and munch long enough to catch them, but they were pretty fast.

They were little parakeets. They rested on a curtain rod; not quite green, they seemed only half ripe. The rest of their bodies was a very light gray. A pair. Their chirps and whistles startled me only because I was used to the deeper, less whimsical sounds of pigeons. —So tiny, I whispered.

—You don't have to keep your voice down, Tony said. They can see us right in front of them.

—Let's think about what we're gonna do, Mark said. He dropped his bag because he needed his hands free to think, to scratch his ears, rub his neck—his body needed that kind of stimulation to work, even during tests. Teachers often thought he was cheating.

Frankie asked, —Couldn't we just throw books at them? I got good aim. And Anthony.

Jung said, —His mother doesn't want dead birds, dick.

Frankie pointed down. —His mother wants what your mother already got: my fat one.

—If we scare them into moving, I said, and we have the other three or four stand close with their bags open I bet we could catch them.

Jung volunteered to be frightening because he had the shortest arms, smallest reach. While he walked forward, slow and crouched, we four raised our bags in the air. The birds were oblivious, hopping two feet to the right with an ease that suggested nothing but absolute stupidity. They burst into joy again and the sound was irritating. Jung pounced and they flew. Like a fire had been lit, they went that fast. I knew I wasn't getting one, thought for sure we'd all missed out, but Mark had his bag closed tight at the top, from inside came a muffled twitter. Tony moved cautiously, saying, —Okay, okay. Just give me that one and I'll put it back.

Mark would not agree so he, Tony and Jung went together into the mother's room.

Frankie looked at me, finally said, —Let me see that hand.

I brought it close to him, he touched the palm and the fingertips. After some more perusal he went to the kitchen, returned with two Korean beers, brown bottles with a gold label, red letters. We drank them though I hated the taste. I couldn't say no to a toast. Then Frankie went to the bookshelf and began tossing paperbacks.

The bird was agitated. It flew by my face and Frankie almost hit me. I joined in. It flitted from pace to place: it dallied at Tony's sneakers, which had been set neatly by the door, their soles worn down from all the running he did in a day. When it landed it dropped its beak down like it was ducking. It flew to the stack of three empty pizza boxes in the living room, sat there as though there was time to reminisce, through the open bathroom door, perched itself on top of the mirror, until I sent an old summer reading copy of *Animal Farm* in there. At the wooden rack on the wall where a string of hats hung, it hopped to the Mets cap, moving one peg left as each of us sent something at it. On the dining-room table was a blue plastic box for clothes, a wash just done—the parakeet stopped there, dug its claws into Tony's mother's bra, a black one, which sat on top. On a stack of red oak tag paper it gave out a significant sound, directed at us. A shattered single note. The parakeet's movements seemed random, bred from confusion, desperate and without any narrative, but when I looked where it had been going I saw that at each station there lay some of those seeds Tony had set out, so few you might not notice from afar. It had been feeding itself; where I'd thought gleefully that we had it on the run, the bird's whole trajectory now seemed deliberate and precise. Mark joined in; Jung pounded against walls to add some noise. We ran out of softcovers after the Bible had gone up; we moved to hardcovers.

Jung then got dinged in the face with a sharp-edged red cookbook and started crying. He was deceptive, you'd see the tears and think he was some big pussy, but once he started swinging his arms like sledgehammers you knew you'd better run because he just might kick your ass. —Alla you get the fuck out of my house! Tony yelled. He turned off the blabbering television.

Mark, Frankie and I were angry to leave without having had some kimchee, jealous that Jung would be allowed to stay like always. As though it had been choreographed, we three bucked out our teeth and pulled our eyes narrow to slits, sang, —Me Chinese, me don't care, me make shitty in my underwear!

In exasperation and some kind of resignation, Tony cried, for him and Jung, —We're not Chinese!

I was laughing so hard that Jung turned to me, said, —I been to your house, Anthony. I don't know what the fuck you're laughing at. I heard your mother talk, she's an African Bootie Scratcher anyway.

I didn't know what he was talking about, but I knew my mother had been insulted and it had to be corrected. —My mother is not some fucking African, she's black.

Mark shrugged. —What's the difference?

Once we were in the hallway, I realized we'd forgotten our bags, banged on Tony's door; reluctantly it opened some, one by one they came out, like sandbags right before a big flood.

We ate gum outside; Frankie had it and shared with me and Mark. I chewed it to hide the beer on my breath. We had a few more blocks to walk together. I saw Olisa before either of them and tried to lead them into the Lug-A-Jug with a promise to buy them Jawbreakers. Frankie peeped her, told me, —Go tell that bitch the facts.

I walked up, the others close enough to hear. We were across the street from a bus stop. Olisa handed me something bright, a maroon paper used for art projects in school; written in orange marker it was hard to see the words ANTHONY-N-OLISA. She asked, —Would you go to a movie with me?

Somewhere in school she'd have heard about my incident. I held that palm up to her face, close, like there was an odor left on it that she could inhale. Nancy Salvino was flat-chested; in her bra I'd felt all that tissue. I said, —Nobody loves your ugly black ass.

She stared at me as I passed. Her mouth divested of words. Her cheeks were round and good, but no one noticed. Frankie and Mark told me to throw her gift away, but I waited until I got home, stuffed it in the garbage near chicken fat and an old wig. I wrapped up the whole bag and took it to the incinerator. Back in the apartment I lay on my bed, spent the rest of the afternoon looking at the hand that had, just that day, touched the thing we thought we'd wanted more than anything else in the world.

how I lost my inheritance

This lawyer was fucking my moms, right in the pocketbook. She was explaining the process to my grandmother as I was splayed out on the floor, staring into the television that was burning through my good eyesight, glasses getting thicker right there on my face. I turned, over my shoulder, shooshed them; they regarded me and laughed out my place in the matriarchy.

My mother asked about school, did it lazily; not that she was uninterested, just so tired. Work produced exhaustion and minor paychecks. She was a secretary. Like many afternoons she'd left me enunciation exercises, not specific phrases for repetition, but a book and radio with a blank tape in the deck. The task was to read clearly into the speaker and she'd listen when evening came to see if I'd done it well. But, like always, she was too tired for her part; knowing this would happen, you'd have thought I could skip it, but Grandma would come to the bedroom door and watch me. One thing I guarantee, throughout Queens no one screamed, —Motherfucker! more clearly than I.

We ate dinner in front of the television. Grandma cooked a meal rich with gravy; as she ate Mom muttered, —I shouldn't be touching this stuff. She rubbed her thighs as though they were expanding right then; she kneaded them with her knuckles in what looked like a punishment. I thought she might take a pill, she seemed agitated enough; she ate some more. Mom touched me where I sat, beside her on the couch, asked, Tomorrow, you want to come with me?

She didn't need to give me a destination. My mother worked so many hours. —Where? I asked.

—I have to see my lawyer. And Grandma needs a break from you.

—You going to make me dress up? I acted indignant; she could have outfitted me in a clown suit if it meant we'd share some time. My mom was much prettier without the wig, her real hair pulled into braids that rose in differing directions when she scratched her scalp, looking to me like thirty-two separate strokes of genius.

—You don't have to dress up, she said. We're meeting him at Burger King.

On Wednesday (or, as I pronounced it, Wed-nes-day) we walked into the Burger King closest to our building. Fifteen blocks, less, five hundred yards from Woolworth's, right next to the Wiz. Mom pulled open the door, said, —Be nice to his man. He has my money and might not give it back.

Burger King was a divided city, two halves, one for teenagers—their bags piled under the tables, hands holding hands or swirling milkshakes, mouths full of curses—the other for adults and, this day, me.

Mr. Law, Mr. Crook, formally known as Cleveland Morris, looked a lot like Lando Calrissian without the perm. He knew his smile worked, it made you forget his shortness, only one word entered my mind: trust. He shook hands correctly, the way my grandmother had already taught me, all firm.

Me and Mom slid together into a booth with a cool orange tabletop. Mr. Morris sat across from us. My hands found the off-white salt shaker, the brown one for pepper; I brought them toward each other at high speed. Crash. And again.

—Stop that. Mom dropped one arm over both of mine.

—So, Miss J——, said her lawyer. What was so urgent?

She dropped her shoulders. —What? I've told you on the phone, in letters, I wanted some kind of report. Progress. She was incredulous.

—I told you it was a long process. These things have many channels. You can't just tell the government to patent an invention and it's done.

My mother had made something worth selling. She had invented it. She was already almost yelling, —I've been working with you for eleven months. I've given you a lot of money. My money. She opened her purse.

He put up his hands. —Now let's try and keep our heads level here.

Mom was not having it; she read to him from a spiral notepad: five hundred dollars on September 18 to retain his services; three hundred dollars on November 11 for a title search; one thousand dollars for a processing fee and hours worked, December 6; one week later, four hundred more for a draftsman to render the product in all its forms and applications, from all angles; just three weeks before this meeting three hundred more for hours logged. She read all this to him, though at each pause for breath he tried to interject an excuse. I listened and thought our family must be rich.

She had a terrible memory; she took diet pills, pink amphetamines with medical names. They worked, so to her the damage they caused was negligible, anything was worth shaving off those pounds that curved out her hips and stomach in a way so American antithetical, like *The Age of Reason* would read to a pope. Her mind was left a mess. It had holes. She might remember a grade she got in school twenty years ago, but not the doctor's appointment next week, not even the doctor's name. It was good she was a secretary, trained to take notes. For appointments, technical things, the birthdays of her son and mother, she kept files, transcripts, memos—meticulous and copious. I often watched her, at night, transcribing the day's jottings from a small notepad to a larger binder she kept beside the couch in the living room.

Mr. Morris smiled. —Your list sounds right.

—My list sounds expensive.

I nodded. Tried to add the figures in my head, but kept losing my place as I enviously spied french fries. I was going to ask Mom for a few dollars but her face was a mixture of concentration and consternation so I made the smart move and kept shut.

—So what did you want to do about things now?

Mom said, —Well, you say you haven't sent in the application yet, right?

—Yes, there are a few more things I want to add. Unless we make it totally specific as to its uses and how it will be packaged, the Patent Office will probably reject it. They demand precision. I don't want to charge you for reapplication, so I'm making sure this one shot has everything they'll need. Then we'll be ready to go.

—Well, that's what I'm thinking about. You told me that if I was ever dissatisfied with how the process was going I could ask you to stop and you'd refund all my money minus the original consultation fee. One hundred forty dollars.

—I said that? He laughed. Are you sure? He pointed at Mom, looked at me. Is your mother playing a joke on me?

I shrugged. Mom leafed to another page in her notebook. —Yes, you said I'd get back all the money except the consultation fee. Would you like to know the date?

—Miss J——, none of this is necessary. What have I done to make you unhappy?

—You took my money and you haven't done your job.

He clicked his teeth, watched my mother, puffed out his cheeks, flickered his fingers over the tabletop. Smiled.

Not working.

—Well, obviously I don't have the money for you now. I wouldn't walk around with that kind of cash.

She sighed. —I wasn't expecting you to. You can mail me a company check or a money order.

—Yes. We could handle the situation that way. But what if I told you I'd work overtime over the next few days and get your application out by the middle of next week and from there I'd have done my job?

—If you could do that now, why couldn't you do that months ago?

—Well, I mean, I didn't know I had such a dissatis-fied customer (smile). It was still going to be ready soon, but now I'll put all my other cases aside and work just for you. What do you think of that?

I got to Mom's bag and plugged my hands into it, found her money purse, clicked it open, dropped all the change on the table, started counting.

—It's too late for that. We're going to have to end this business.

He seemed unfazed; had this been me, I would have had the ache of losing all that money bursting from my forehead and over my eyes, down into my mouth, but he was showing none of that and I was thinking maybe this was why he was an adult. He agreed to meet us there again in a few days; my mother suggested we make it two. He slid out, left without looking back-ward.

Mom gave me bills to replace the three dollars I'd amassed from her coin vault. I bought some fries, knew without being told to bring her a coffee and three pack-ets of Sweet 'n Low, a spoon. I sat across from her. She looked around. —Do you come here sometimes?

—Nah. Who comes in here?

She shrugged. —There are teenagers right over there.

—They're like fourteen, fifteen. They'd kick my ass.

—What was that?

—Butt.

—Right. She looked. Any of those boys over there?

—What?

—The ones who bother you.

I laughed the way a native speaker does when a foreigner clumsily attempts his language. —They don't do anything. I'm just saying, if I came in here they would.

She nodded but had no idea. —You sure you're not embarrassed to be seen out with your Mum?

You can't tell your parents when they've made you happy. I faked a weary tone. —I guess I don't mind.

She sipped her coffee after she had added the chemicals to make it palatable; she drank even with the steam rushing up. —I know you're eleven and all, so I thought you might feel too grown for this. With me.

Mom liked to put herself in a historical context, to teach me something. She felt awful being absent often and hoped in some way that knowledge might take her place. She compared having me to taming the Wild West. When she and my dad divorced (I was one)? The fight for separation of church and state. And now, battling this lawyer? The fight with the U.S. Government for control of the Black Hills. (I had to do the research myself each time, come home and try to explain my mother's logic—the last, Black Hills, went like this: the money, her invention, they were hers by all natural rights but through chicanery and loopholes it was being kept somewhere just out of reach; she could see the distant mountain ranges, but it seemed impossible again to climb that glorious terrain.)

A day after our Burger King excursion I came back from school to find my mother home early. I couldn't even take off my coat before she pulled me to the bathroom, sat me on the toilet. The room was cluttered with a mop, two buckets, bottles of tile cleaners and sheets of plastic.

—What stinks? I asked.

She smiled broadly, pulled a scarf around her head. —I've been trying out all these cleaners, comparing which does the best job.

—Why?

—You've never seen my invention, have you? I mean noticed it.

—Where would I see it?

She touched the walls in the bathtub, behind a curtain of green. —Here it is.

I laughed. —You invented walls?

She rubbed her thumb over some of the peach-colored tiles. —These things collect dirt. If you had to clean them you'd notice that. But I haven't cleaned them in a year. Because of this. She pulled at a corner above her head and peeled down a thin layer of plastic that had been invisible to me. She stopped after some of it stuck out like an enormous tongue.

She said, —I came up with this idea over the years. Let me show you how I want the commercial to go! She was instantly joyous; she was a person who could really get into things, you know the kind, who can be so happy you swear they're fucking with you, but they mean it.

—Have you ever been in the bathroom, scrubbing and scrubbing at these tiles and cried, Can't there be a better way? Used all the cleaners. Sprayed, scrubbed, sprayed, scrubbed, sprayed, scrubbed and sweated? Doesn't do anything for the walls and oh! the way your fingers ache. But now! The brilliant minds of Moms Incorporated have created the Tile Defender! She paused. Guardian of your pristine walls. Simply apply the precut sheets, either in original Clear or decorated with tasteful designs to liven up your lavatory!

—And what does it do, madam? Grandma asked from the hallway, in the semi-English she spoke, a little late for her part. They had been rehearsing that one line for a week, though until now I hadn't known why. The first time my grandmother had tried to repeat the question, hard of hearing and language barriered, she'd asked my mom, And what does it do, madman?

We worked well together: Mom gave the pitch, Grandma feigned the innocent bystander and I was the unsuspecting dupe. As Mom ran through her lines a second and third time, Grandma and I stayed in character. We laughed and I thought my mother's only career should be inventing, it seemed to allow so much more joy than that office in Manhattan. As she wound down the last time, she spread her arms, breathing heavy from the acting. Grandma clapped and I joined in; my mother bowed and accepted the praise.

Then Friday afternoon found Mom and I off to collect money. She was working only full-time while she handled this business, not the extra hours she was allowed many evenings.

In front of the Wiz were friends of mine. The store blasted hits to tempt passersby, entice a purchaser inside. Instead they got kids like me leaning against the glass, chewing gum and learning all the words for free. They were respectful, my friends, when we reached them. Mom let me socialize while she spoke with a woman she'd run into, someone small whom I saw at the occasional family picnic.

—Your mom making you get clothes? Cindac asked, his giant chin moving as he ground gum between the teeth.

I told him, —We're going to Burger King.

—Yeah, he replied.

Mom laughed with her friend. There were four boys watching the Walkmans on display, counting me. We were all eleven. They had a way, these store owners, of making the cheapest thing seem precious by virtue of a little gray stand and some colored paper behind an item. My mother's words grew louder to fight the traffic, volume enough to reach us, for one kid to cock his head and ask, —What the fuck is she saying?

I turned, assuming he was speaking of someone else, but then he had to point at my mother. —What do you mean? I asked, listening, hearing nothing I didn't hear often in our home.

—It's not Spanish, Cindac snapped. I tell you that. He laughed. They speaking some fucking Martian shit. He looked at me. Where the fuck is your family from?

—Uganda.

—What?

—Uganda.

—Where is that? one boy yelled, genuinely perplexed, angry at the confusion.

I shrugged, went to my mother, interrupted and asked, returned, too stupefied by her answer to lie. —Africa, I said.

They laughed so hard it sounded like bad coughs. My mother even turned. For my part, my head dropped with the shame; who cares what color your neighborhood, in 1983, New York, it was no good being an African. Black people were Americans, Africans were some other, weird shit. The only thing as bad was Haitian. It was a rule somewhere, kids knew this.

—So your mother doesn't take baths. They don't wash, right?

There was agreement, heads nodded, even mine.

—And they eat shit raw. Hunt their food.

I stopped agreeing with them, but I didn't think they were actually wrong. Wasn't that all Africans did? What we'd been told? Told one another? It was like, for some other kind of kid, realizing that first time that your father is not the Ruler, but the Ruled; it's the first time you get those new eyes.

My mother came for me, smiled at my friends, who waved. Cindac called out, —We'll talk with you later. I anticipated the beatdown to come, but was not actually scared. When Mom held the door open for me I watched her callused fingertips, the uneven, bitten-down nails. Cleveland Morris had already taken a seat. In front of him was a folder, important looking and emerald green.

Mom said hello and I nodded at the crook, she smacked my head lightly and I made a better greeting. This time I wasn't waiting for the whole ceremony. I tapped Mom on the ear. Tapping. Finally she broke.
—What?!

—A shake.

—Do you want a shake?

—Of course Mom.

—Then ask me.

—Mother?

—Yes?

—May I please trouble you if it's not too much bother to afford me the money so that I may purchase a vanilla shake?

She sighed, but smiled. —One minute Mr. Morris.

He didn't care, even offered to pay, but they were well past small niceties. When I returned, her mouth was open—agape; for years I pronounced this a-ga-pay. She was silent, he spoke. Explained that he'd gone ahead and submitted the application, done all he'd been hired for; this, he assured my mother, was a good thing. But Mom had a habit of wanting people to listen to her, so she lost her temper, loud then louder. I was leaning against the table, but took a step back so this lawyer could get the whole barrage. He leaned backward, wishing for bullets to come through the front window, a grease fire. No luck.

Then she was gesticulating. I had no sympathy for her, people were looking. An African could not control itself, this was her son's thinking. Her hand shot out and sent his hot coffee up, landing across our boy Cleveland.

—Shit, woman! he yelled, tried to stand, but got corralled by the tabletop, which caught him in the yams. Back down, he rubbed his face, lifted that folder, shook it; random droplets flecked out in six directions.

—I want all your paperwork, showing me what you say you did for all that money. I'll report you. That I was cheated.

He shook his face. —You do what you like. You'll hear from the Patent Office about approval or not in a few weeks. I've done my job. He rose, taking the folder with him, having never presented its contents. He seemed to be taunting her, implying that what she wanted was so near; with the hand that held it, Cleveland Morris waved good-bye.

Mom shut her eyes, began talking to herself, throwing hands wild enough to conduct an orchestra. Anytime before this afternoon, I'd have talked her calm, slowly assuring her things would be fine; it had been my job to do this on occasion. Other people laughed at her exhibition and I was mortified, disgusted. I stepped back, one foot. She looked up at the menu, white numbers on a black background, pictures flanking either side. —I haven't had one of those fish fillets in so long.

I shook my head for her. Besides soothing her, I was meant to bolster her will when necessary. —You're not really hungry, Mom.

She grabbed my arm like we were going to fight, that hard, then released. —You're right. You're right. Her purse opened and out came the pills. I was embarrassed, suddenly sure that to all the other customers she was now not only the Angry African, but also heavy, her slim form before them only an act. Temporary.

—Mom, I groaned, people are looking.

She opened her mouth, for more volume. —You think I care what these people are thinking? I will speak whenever I please.

My head sank; let some revolutionary someone else

be proud of the Unsilenced Woman. From another
table I retrieved napkins, brought the stack over and
dropped it on what was left of the spill. Mom spoke to
no one. We were both learning to rely more on ourselves. I pushed my hands down until I could feel the
moistness on my palms, then swished the papers
around, sopping up all the brown wet.

Cleveland Morris had bosses. My mother tracked
them down. Their office stood eleven blocks from our
building, closer even than the Burger King. On Monday, she and I went. We stopped outside and Mom
leaned against a wall, turned her face up and told herself not to be afraid. I rubbed the back of her hand half-
heartedly.

In a seven-story building, their offices took up the
entire sixth floor. She and I were shuffled into a waiting
room; judging by the masses, we were on a very long
line. Many women slept with their faces against their
purses, leaning that far forward. The chairs were of all
types: wooden with no backs, metal folding chairs,
bright yellow plastic welded four to a frame. Men stood
and paced then sat and huffed. No one was happy. People talked, conversations kept private by the loud rzzzz
of the giant old fan spitting dust from a corner.

—So you want to know about Africa?

I wanted to quiet her. She watched me expectantly,
as though I had questions rehearsed; our chairs seemed
farther apart, a cause for both celebration and sadness. I

put my hand out to touch her arm and pulled it back. I blew out air. I was confused.

We sat quietly, waiting just to make an appointment to be heard about Mom's complaint. Mom took down the name of the woman who put us in the date book, the woman who seemed personally offended when my mother mentioned the words "small claims court." I drew a picture of her big fat head on a sheet of paper that had been lying on the floor.

We returned on a Thursday. Mom brought me straight from school, rode a public bus overpopulated with the young. I dipped my head down as we traveled together. In the rear Cindac was yelling, —African Anthony! then ducking so my mother wouldn't see who'd screamed.

Then us in the waiting room, sneaking into a spot I didn't like because three rows of people sat behind me—having people behind you, that's how spitballs got in your hair. Mom asked if my old sneakers were too old. I blurted out, —You should have stayed there.

—Where? She had been going over the delineation of grievances she'd prepared the night before.

—Uganda. I mouthed the word out, barely a whisper that no one else could hear. We could have just been living there, doing fine. I doubted very much that it was so shameful to be African in Africa.

But my mother had her own logic and reasoning and when I suggested she could have done better for her boy she twisted her lower lip like she'd suddenly been stabbed. She grabbed my right arm at the elbow, squeezed, said, —You don't know anything.

It didn't actually hurt, but I winced regardless. —Get off me. I pulled free.

She tugged her wig down; it was cut with unflattering bangs. —The very last time I visited, she said, you were eight. You remember? I was gone for two months?

Nodding, I said, —Nineteen eighty. That year, I was skipped a grade. My family hadn't treated it ceremoniously.

She rubbed a thumb against her chin, just below the lip, like memories were stored there, like she could jiggle them loose; in her head they were slightly incongruous, trickling out in odd arrangements.

In fact, she remembered very little, only that a cousin named Franklin met her at the airport, that she'd brought along all our old clothes for family. I interjected that maybe this was where my Spider-Man T-shirt had gone, but, of course, she could not recall. Sixteen-year-old boys who had been given guns and called soldiers sat at checkpoints and jabbed their muzzles into any woman who passed. At a small club my mother danced to Percy Sledge. The land, she told me, was beautiful with hills. Unlike New York, in Uganda the weather was a blessedly dry heat, you were not grimy at the end of a day.

—At the airport I went six hours early. I had confirmed the ticket in New York and Nairobi; the woman at the ticket counter gave me trouble; she wanted a bribe; I'd been away so long I had forgotten how things worked; we yelled at each other. I missed my plane. She said I'd made a mistake but Franklin was sure she'd sold my seat to someone who knew how to pass a tip. At the airport, as I was panicking, I ran into a friend, Lucy. Lucy had gone to King's College Budo with me.

—I thought you went to college in Canada, I interrupted.

—It's called King's College, but it's a grade school. Listen:

Lucy offered to make the very long drive from Entebbe to Nairobi before her husband had said yes; he was standing there, obviously angry, but was a little man and took any responsibility very seriously. She had only been bumped from the Entebbe to Nairobi journey and, if they made it in time, she was assured there was still a place on the connecting flight to London and from there, America.

Lucy had two little girls; her husband owned two cars. A cousin of theirs acted as chauffeur for Lucy and the kids in return for a room, so he could live in a city. The girls wore dresses nice enough for a confirmation and bright, black shoes. They ate little cakes, cheered when they were told of the long ride. Their noses looked almost like mine.

As they got out into the country, the two men raced. Mom rode with the husband. In the other car the girls used the bumps in the road to excuse their hopping around. They were scuffing up the seats and enjoying themselves. At times the cars were close and Mom could hear them scream, Sorry Mummy! They threw their hands up and laughed like it was a roller coaster. Lucy's husband was a better driver, the other car trailed, soon they were gone. Lucy's husband wanted to wait but Mom showed him her ticket, the flight time. Mom cried a little and not every tear was genuine. They arrived almost an hour early. She gave him fifty dollars, but he refused. Mom told him to buy his girls some pastries with the money, but he told her it was Lucy who indulged them. Then he took the money anyway.

Mom called Franklin days later to ask him to send her some things she'd forgotten. He told her that Lucy's husband had returned to find the other car parked by the road, empty. He had opened all the doors, inspected the boot. Not even blood. He came back with police whom he paid to make a genuinely thorough search. Lucy, both girls and his cousin left nothing. Franklin told Mom this and she was shocked, mute, but was not sad. She'd have urged him to keep driving even if she'd known what was going to happen to his family. She had to leave, it was no longer her home. Mom asked after Lucy for two more years and each time Franklin had no good word. There couldn't even be a burial. She'd have sent a few dollars for some kind of ceremony. Mom cried sometimes and Grandma told her not to feel guilt, but it wasn't that, it was relief and it was joy. She was thankful she had me in Manhattan. Regardless of who was sacrificed, Mom thanked God.

I was kicking my feet forward and back in my chair; she was breathing heavy and close to tears. I barely noticed. I asked, —So did you ever make it to the airport? I smiled.

She made a noise, sucked her teeth in disgust, so loud that other people looked back, thinking she was commenting on the long wait. They nodded.

We were called into an office with a woman and three men, Mr. Morris among them. There was an air in the room not of apology, but attrition.

The woman wore small gold earrings but the lobes were long, they flapped as she reached for the folder and slid it forward. Mom flipped it open, leafed through sheets. —What is this?

—Everything, the woman said. All our paperwork, your initial information and your check. We have withdrawn your application for a patent. You may work with someone else.

A fan hung from the ceiling, three flat flower petals on the end of an upturned stem. Paint on the walls had been faded by sunlight into a diamond pattern. Behind these four a window was open, the other was closed, a

blind drawn over it so that the wall seemed to be wink-
ing at us, telling Mom, You won.

—Is that it?

They all wore cheap clothes, suits, the woman in her
dress. The money they made was not going to their
wardrobes. One man with eyes that stuck out like a
frog's asked, —What else do you want? Should Mr.
Morris have to shine you shoes?

They had given my mother the materials she
wanted, but damn, this was some shit and even I knew
it. These people knew how to cheat and who. They ran
television commercials on Sundays during *Like It Is*.
All these brown lawyers would get on the screen and
make it sound progressive, political and positive: Black
lawyers for Black clients, Latino lawyers for Latino
clients; they had descended on us. It was a lesson many
of these people were learning: we can't even trust one
another. She grinned at Cleveland Morris and waved
her papers in the air. —This is mine.

In our apartment Grandma overjoyed loudly at her
daughter's triumph. We ate dinner together, laughed as
Mom mimed Mr. Morris's morose manner. Then, next
day, Mom returned to overtime, back to our routine.

I spent the next three weeks trying to coax her into
some shared action: shopping for clothes, getting
Grandma a gift for her birthday five months away. Let's
just do something, was my mantra. She'd sit on the
couch, appreciative but exhausted and tell me that the

little time she had would be spent on the Tile Defender—recopying notes, sending packets out to other patent lawyers. She'd explain this to me and ask, —Do you understand?

I did. I hated her. Wistfully I remembered the Burger King lounge like it had been the site of some historic event. Somehow she needed to be persuaded to work with me again.

Visited the three spots in our home: beside the couch in the living room, the filing cabinet in our shared bedroom, the cupboard above the stove where she had a strongbox, never locked. I took the proper papers from all three: the lists of ingredients, all the legal notations Mr. Morris had made (he had done a little), even the script for the commercial that she'd typed up. Brought them to the stove while my grandmother was taking a furious shit.

The front right burner clicked then blew a blue flame out into a halo. I rolled all the sheets into a thick, uneven cone, held them over the fire. I don't say this was all in the hopes of re-creating a partnership; I also thought jealously of the good things in Uganda: dry heat, families with the money for two cars, hilly green terrain and even Percy Sledge. To me, she'd only mentioned these things to make me envious, at the time it was all I'd heard. I thought she'd cheated me; not of money, but your family, your home; they're also things to inherit.

As they burned I ran the blackening pages under tap water until a height of charred, soaking ash was left. I ran more water as the paper slowly drained down the sink. I opened a window. No one came into the kitchen for a while, Grandma was occupied, so the smell had time to leave, out the window, mingling with pigeons and pedestrians.

Mom was frantic that night. She ran into our room, where I lay on my bed reading a comic, my feet folded under me. She asked if I'd seen her papers, checked the orange filing cabinet someone had been throwing away at her office, the one she'd brought home on the 7 train, the one I'd cleaned and smoothed the dents out of for three dollars. Nothing. She turned, asked quietly, —Have you seen my papers?

—I saw them, I told her, dropped my comic.

—Where are they? Despite her volume, her face was not as angry as I thought it would be; there was desperation, there was sadness. I tried to think which reason she'd rather hear: the blame or the adoration. Grandma was in another room, asking in Luganda and English if anything had been found.

Mom and I sat on the edge of my bed; this is how we perched when she read me books as a little boy, *Peter and the Wolf* was my favorite. —This is what I was thinking, Mom. If you didn't have those papers I could help you do the work again. We could choose another lawyer. I could help you buy the sheeting, cut it up, put on the adhesive. I could be your assistant.

—Where are the papers? She enunciated every word.

—And if we worked together you could tell me more stuff.

—The papers?

—I burned them.

She nodded; her next question seemed to come from genuine curiosity. —Do you hate me that much?

I watched her feet. —Yes.

—Kitchen, she commanded.

Grandma had gone off to her room, from where I could hear the vacuum cleaner going, high-power. Mom sat, then spoke, —Bread, marmalade, knife. I got each, brought them, forgot the plate but she didn't notice. She twisted open the bag of bread and dropped every slice on the table.

The marmalade was half gone. Inside, the orange strings and clear jam coated the jar. She unscrewed the cap with one long twist strong enough for the top to bounce off, onto the table and down to the floor, it spun as it came to a stop.

She mashed the marmalade into the bread until the middle curved in, then she spread it as best she could. Small tears appeared and the fake wood beneath showed through. She ate sloppily, but didn't make any noise. She still chewed with a closed mouth. Her back, as she breathed, bent into a 'c,' her head hanging somewhere near mine. I looked into her face, its burdens. When her hand came up I thought she was going to punch me, the walls seemed ready for it, but my mom wasn't a violent person, even now; her fist didn't know that and it waited there, near me, like it was making up its own mind. She said, —Maybe this really isn't working out. Someone may have to come for you.

You should've seen our wallpaper. Not what had been there when we moved in, I don't even remember that one, the new one, put up on an energetic Saturday when she had roped me and Grandma in, getting the boy to peel off and cut the right-size strips while the old lady sat near the oven with a pot of glue coming to a simmer for spreading. The bare walls had had blemishes, remainders of the families before. That they had gone on to something else was not the only interesting part. We also talked of the next tenants who might, while redecorating, press a palm to the surface and, in so doing, imagine our lives.

pops

My father was eating pizza across from me, sucking in cheese and smiling like we were family. I was eleven and felt five. The fans overhead moved slow and uneven like drunks. If I was shorter I would have been swinging my feet.

—You're good looking, my dad told me like he was surprised.

—I am?

—Sure, sure. You look like your mother.

The pizza was extra good, pepperoni slid down the

slice on an easy river of grease; I ate each red circle one by one. The Italian guy behind the counter, taking money and making friends, had jokes with me when we'd bought our food. I'd laughed extra hard because I was too damn nervous.

—So, what's your first name? I asked him.

His face didn't know how to deal with me. —Louis.

—Your name is Louis?

—Uh-huh.

—Louis J—— I blew out the name like bubbles, it made my lips numb.

—Do you like it?

—The pizza?

—My name.

—No.

He bit more slice, swallowed and asked me why.

—I beat up a kid named Louis.

—On your own? He raised his shoulders like I was making him happy.

—No, I said. Me and my friends. We kicked his ass. I waited to see if he was the kind of guy to blow his dick out if I cursed a little. My mom was like that. He didn't squawk.

—What did Louis do?

—I don't know, I said. I had made the whole thing up.

—You remember when I saw you a few years ago? he asked me.

—You never been to see me.

—That's true, he said.

The front door kept opening and closing, jingling its bells. People were hungry, but I wasn't. I took another chew, drank some soda. Sprite. —How old are you? I looked at his face; it was big and not too pretty, but something about him was nice. I could see him being trusted.

—I'm almost forty. Thirty-nine and looking good. This was my dad, wearing the Yankee cap he'd bought for me, the one I didn't want. He'd made the purchase after saying hello and good-bye to my mother.

—What do you do? I asked him.

—For a living?

—Okay.

—Well, when I was with your mother I was teaching. High school, grade school. Whatever.

—What subject?

—I did math a lot but really I taught biology.

I was impressed, duke sitting across from me, looking like a broke-ass Al Pacino, had taught the subjects I'd be failing soon. He leaned forward. —How do you think you'd do in one of my classes? Are you a good student?

—No.

He sat back, stretched his arms, crossed them. —Why not?

—Bad teachers.

He laughed; he sounded like a little girl, like me and my friends when we got joking.

—You still teaching? I asked him.

He shook his head. —No.

—Can I get another slice? I asked. He bought me one. I watched him at the counter, he was good at being social. He leaned forward when he spoke so it seemed like he was only talking to you. When he sat he was quick with the answer to my next question.

—I'm a police officer.

Whatever words were planning to pop out next stuck up in my throat and made me cough.

—Surprised? he asked.

—Scared.

Pops nodded. —Okay.

I whispered, —So you have your gun on you?

—No.

—Why not?

—Just don't, he said. I'm a cop in Connecticut, not around here.

—Where's that?

He lifted his arm and pointed over my shoulder. —There.

—How far from here?

—Maybe an hour.

Funny that this dude who had disappeared on me was enforcing laws in another state.

—You ride around in a car or what? I was feeling less

scared of my man; he had been huge when he'd shown up at our apartment amazingly, but he was not as universal as before. The ovens were sweating out their heat; I kept my jacket on. My father slid his off and wiped that skull; this was an endurance test.

—Yeah, he said. I ride a car and I have a partner.

—Your partner's black?

—No.

—If he was then you two could be like *I Spy*.

He nodded. —Sure.

—I was in a play, I told him.

—So you're an actor?

—No.

—What play was it?

I started and stopped because my chin was begging for some napkins. I cleaned myself off then explained. —A scene from *Return of the Jedi*.

—The *Star Wars* movies, right?

—You got it, I told him, pointed right at his face.

—So what did you do?

—I was Darth Vader.

—With the mask?

—Uh-huh. And I got my mom to buy me a real good one. It was heavy and came apart like the real one. But it was hot.

—Did it look good?

—Of course it looked good. That mask was like thirty dollars!

—Thirty dollars? He tried to whistle. Pretty expensive.

—Yeah.

—And your mom didn't mind getting it?

—Are you kidding? She went crazy! She was screaming, Thirty dollars! Thirty dollars! Grandma told her not to get it.

—Yeah, your grandmother doesn't like spending that money.

He knew. I laughed. Then him. —Sometimes, I said. Sometimes I ask Grandma for some money to get a comic and she tells me to read the ones I have, but I've read them ten times! I leaned forward; the walls of the pizza place were hard to hate—Dave Winfield was signed, framed and posing, swinging on a nail. Next to him? Craig Nettles.

—Your mother and me were dating once, this was before you were born.

Ah-duh, I thought.

—And man, I showed up to take your mother out for some dinner, but your grandmother wanted me to come in. You know, say hello, all that stuff. So I came in and she served me some tea. We drank that for a little while.

—Too much milk in the tea? I asked.

—That's your grandma. So we finish and we've talked for a while and your mom comes out ready to go, looking great as usual. Man, I'm telling you, your mom was the best-looking black lady I ever saw. I mean she had those hips and . . . well, so your grandmother, she takes our cups and sits there, while I'm watching, she sits there draining out what's left of the tea; then she collects the little grounds that are left at the bottom of the cup and drops them on a napkin. So I'm sitting there thinking, what is this? And your mom tells me later that your grandmother reuses the grounds. She gets about three cups where us mortals would get one.

We laughed because he had my grandmother down solid, seemed like he was going to pop into imitating the way she held her neck. I stopped, but money was laughing so hard his balls had to be hurting. I was smiley for another minute, then I got angry. —Stop laughing at my grandmother.

He was heaving; it wasn't as funny as all that. —I'm sorry Anthony. I'm sorry.

—Then stop.

—Okay.

But he didn't and I sat watching until he got rid of all the humor in his lungs.

—So you done with that pizza?

I was, but half the slice was there on my plate. I didn't want to waste it, but I didn't feel hungry anymore. I killed what was left of the soda and told him I was ready to be out. We moved for the door. Teenagers were cramped into a booth and smoking at one another. I was sad because I liked the smell of cooking cheese, but the right thing to do seemed to be to get going. Outside it was four in the afternoon.

—You want to go home? my father asked.

I looked down the block, past the Korean market where the fruit was sitting out on green wooden stands; grandmothers were clawing at the produce. Two blocks away was my apartment building and a game of punchball or tag. I looked at this guy. —I don't have to go yet.

His face was plain, he nodded extra-happy; we walked together. Across the street was the place where I got my glasses, where they welded those plastic-framed tortures to my skull. When we had gone about a block my father stopped. —What? I asked.

He was looking down at me, there was a grin. —Your mother ever tell you about me?

—No. I never ask.

He laughed, trying not to seem embarrassed. —Aren't there some pictures of me around or anything?

I stepped backward, leaned against a building so we weren't entertaining others in the middle of the side-walk. He followed. —There's one picture of you, I said.

—Where is it?

—In a drawer.

—What's the picture of? He kicked at the building with one foot.

—It's when you and Mom got married.

—Oh yeah? Do I look nice in it?

—You both do, I told him and they did. There are things a son is supposed to ask his father, but I didn't know what they were; his swinging shoe was coming closer and closer to a tidy pile of dog shit. I didn't tell him even when he went right through it. He didn't notice. I laughed.

—What's funny?

I pointed.

—You want to see a movie? He was running the toe of his shoe against the building to try and clean it off; I always tore off leaves and used them to wipe it all away.

Cars were babbling from Kissena Boulevard to Franklin Avenue, their horns loud and angry; I liked the specific music of Flushing traffic, it told me I was home. Then, sounds like these existed only in the piece of city where I lived.

—I don't want to see any movies, I told him. I didn't want to be in the dark with this man because I was friendlier to everyone when a room was one big shadow. I felt comforted and sure when the lights were out. There's a park nearby. Sometimes I play basketball there.

—I'm too old for basketball.

—Not to play it, but there's benches there. We could sit down.

He followed me, stopped only once to run into a corner store, came out with a brown bag. —Just something we need.

At the park the black iron gates were shut so I took my father around to the wonderful hole in the fence; I slid through easy, he took more time. Once inside, we passed kids making teams for basketball. The green benches had been repainted so they looked perfect and new. I stopped my dad from sitting, ran my hands gentle across the seats until I found one where very few splinters grew; the new paint was like camouflage, laid out like that to fool the eye. New benches were expensive. The ground in the park was old and dying concrete.

—You know where I grew up? he asked me.

—Greenland?

He laughed. —Why would you say Greenland?

—Okay. Iceland?

—No, no. Neither one.

—Lapland?

—You know the names of those places but you don't know where Connecticut is? He laughed some more.

—I only know about interesting places. Like Uganda.

—Connecticut is interesting.

I gave him that look I had, the yeah-right look, and he nodded wildly.

—Seriously. There's a lot of interesting things about Connecticut.

—Name fourteen, I said.

He had been sitting up straight as he protested about his new home state, but then he sat back again, defeated. —Fourteen?

—Sure. Why not? I could tell you fourteen great things about Uganda.

He got in my face like these were the kinds of challenges that mattered. —Name one.

—It's not Connecticut.

He smiled proudly. —I knew you couldn't.

If I hadn't known better, I would have thought this was one of my friends, getting his chest puffed out when he proved someone else wrong or stupid. But this was my father and I couldn't just laugh it off. —The capital of Uganda is Kampala. The flag has a white-crested crane on it and the chief mining product is copper.

My dad acted unimpressed, but he was quiet for more than a minute. —So where'd you learn all that?

—Comic book.

—You read a comic book about Uganda?

—Yes.

—Really?

—Yeah, I said and rolled my eyes.

—You sure?

—Okay, maybe I did a report.

He pointed at me. —See, I knew you were a good student.

—I am not, I protested. I'd only recently acquired this interest in some of my ancestry.

—Bet you do really well, he said. The smile on his face seemed too wide for his lips, but there it was— pride. Like he had something to do with it.

—Okay, maybe I'm a good student. I'm just not that smart.

He rubbed his hands through his messy straight hair.

—Maybe that's what I got from you. We both were quiet and tense. So you never told me where you were from.

He began talking over the distant hum of our isolation. —I was born in Syracuse.

—Where?

—Upstate. About six hours, maybe five if you've got a quick bus driver.

—You lived on a farm?

—No, he laughed. Syracuse is a city. Just like New York, but smaller.

I had at least one stupid thing to say, but decided to let the old guy talk.

—You get beat up a lot? he asked me.

His asking me was a reminder that some people live with the idea of getting beaten up instead of doing the beating. —No.

—I used to get beat up all the time. I mean I would get my ass kicked. Big time.

—Who were you pissing off?

—Oh, everybody. Everyone that might beat me up, they did. My father used to tell me to find a way to deal with it, my mother taught me how to fight.

—Did it help?

—No.

The sounds of traffic began to echo in the air. —So did you run away from home or something? Get out of Syracuse?

—No. He tapped his hands on his knees, but he was half a beat off whatever he was trying to get at.

—You smoke? he asked me.

—Not yet.

—Okay. Well, that's what I did for a while. Smoked, drank.

—Did it help?

—Yes. People stopped beating me up because I wasn't in school so much anymore.

I laughed. —I hope you never told this story to your students.

—No. Just you. And your mother.

—What did she say when you told her?

—She said, Buy me another drink and tell me again.

—My mother doesn't drink.

We looked at each other for the first time since we'd sat down. —You're right, he said. I was only joking.

—So how'd you become a teacher?

—I don't know. Sooner or later you grow up.

I wanted to laugh, but then he'd think he'd said

something right. I pointed between his feet. —What's in the bag?

—Well, I figured we might not see each other for a while.

—Yeah.

He revealed a six pack of beer. —I thought you should be able to say you had a drink with your dad.

I looked at the cool white cans with their bright red lettering; I thought I understood what sentiment my father was trying for. I appreciated it.

The sky was the oily gray of shark fins now, people were heading indoors. The handball court was empty; the kids playing basketball had grabbed up their shirts and balls, were filing out through the broken spot in the fence. Someone had left a pair of sneakers under a backboard. The toes curled upward—they were old shoes but their bright blue skin stood out like life on a desolate planet.

He handed me a beer and asked if I'd ever had any.

—I've had some here and there, I told him. I swallowed.

—Chug that down, my father said.

I looked at him and he was smiling, finished off his first.

—You drink that fast and we'll be done with these beers in five minutes, I said.

He petted the bag. —I bought two six packs.

I nodded, drank some more. I hated the taste of beer

like I hated giving relatives hugs, but I was used to both. I was going to ask him some other things, history things—about him and my mom and me.

Finished my beer and tapped his leg. My father gave me the next one. He was so laid back it seemed as though his body had melted into the bench. I looked the same. He smiled as he drank; like always I grimaced as I forced myself to swallow. The man reached out to touch my shoulder or my face but hesitated when he got close, let his hand fall back to his lap; I pretended that drinking beer had left me oblivious.

—You're going to get sick in this bad weather, I told him.

—You too.

—But if I get sick I miss school, there's nothing bad about that.

He leaned close to me. —Nothing wrong with missing a little work either.

He had finished two beers and was halfway through his third; I had killed one and was almost done with the next.

—You think your mom might be around later?

—What for?

The hand rose again, like to touch me but it was on himself, running his hair neat. —I'm not leaving for two more days. You think your mother might want some dinner?

Then, like it happens, bad skies got better; sunlight

started making things nice, nice, nice. Right away people showed up on the streets again; kids were on their way back to the park. My father checked his watch. I got two more, handed him one and popped the other, but we had done all the drinking we were going to do.

His laugh came out like a shout. I asked why.

—You know, one time, when I was still with your mother?

I kept shut because I had never known that era.

—I remember we did it once, finished, and she wanted to go again. Right there. Didn't even have time to wipe the juice off.

I shrugged, it was all the move I could manage.

—It's getting late, he said.

It wasn't.

His face was all lit up, call it glee.

—And? I asked.

—We should get back to your mom. He stretched his arms like he could reach her from here.

kids on colden street

This was the year of crib deaths. This was the year of baby sisters. Our newborn, named Nabisase, cried even after she was fed. My mother came home weak from her labors. Grandma was the dishwasher and a pessimist. And then there was me.

Flushing had come alive in a wave of infants. You'd have thought there was a block-wide blackout nine months before. Our building leaned left with all the new weight on our side; at the other end of the place the elderly were not propagating. Diapers and bottles came in like a relief effort. When the elevator was broken, supplies were hauled up stairs on the scarred legs of older brothers. This was a change for most of us, this was a very new thing.

Each boy had ways to handle it. The standard was indifference. Ray and Bertram did this. Ali took it another route and ran. At twelve that seemed stupid, but he'd always been good with people so he took a chance. Between other conversations we would imagine where he had gone.

I became a family man.

Todd brought me to his third-floor apartment, on a Monday. He lived in one of the strip-thin homes that larger buildings like mine bracketed. We climbed past boxes, bikes left on landings. His mother was at work, his older sister too, cashiering at Key Food. His mother was distant and tall, a skinny woman who never let him have visitors. His long, swinging hair was a family trait, superblond; Todd's skin was so pale we had to call him Red.

Todd, his sister and his mother had their own rooms. I shared one with my mother and our new girl. This arrangement wasn't deadly yet: I hadn't started having those dreams that left me needing privacy, waking up with messy sheets.

—What is it? I asked, annoyed at the buildup. I have something to show you, that's all he'd said.

Todd opened the door to his room, told me to wait inside. His room was how a boy's should be: a mess. A week of clothes on the floor, piles of the unwashed. I sat on the bed, that old Space Shuttle–style frame, a short mattress in the middle. I only came up to Todd's shoulder and this thing was too small for me. On the end where his ankles would droop his mother had wrapped the thick yellow cushioning that televisions came in before Styrofoam. I stared at the material, getting bored; it was so perfect I couldn't help but pick at it until fingerfulls were at my feet like baby chicks on a farm. Todd stepped in. —What the fuck are you doing? He tossed me a ball good for running bases, stickball or handball. I squeezed it.

He left again, shut the door. That Thurman Munson poster was still hanging there, on tacks. Todd talked about it incessantly. In it, Thurman was watching something he'd swatted over a fence, standing straight like he wouldn't run until he'd heard the ball bounce down Bronx streets. The look on his face might have been called intensity but it had been a few years since he'd been in that crash, so to me he seemed to be listening to those game-day clouds as they whispered, You're going to die up here. Todd's father had left this for him before catching a plane back to Sweden where he lived apart from all he'd made here; somehow, fathers were leaving all types of things behind with which their sons might remember them, objects over which we could obsess.

Todd pushed open the door, in his right hand a small peach-colored box; with his left he turned on the light. He sat next to me, opened the box, turned it over and dropped the diaphragm onto his palm. It looked like half a rubber ball.

—That's it?

—Oh yeah, Todd said. He held it over his mouth and nose. Look, a surgeon's mask.

Laughing for no reason, I asked, —How does it work?

—My sister puts it in her pussy and it catches the guy's cum so she won't get pregnant.

I looked at him like he was stupid.

—I swear.

I put my hands out, he tossed it to me. —In her pussy? I asked, then, to my nose with it.

—She hasn't used it yet, asshole.

I kept it over my face, trying to imagine. I threw it back to Todd.

—But that's not the best part. See the little holes? He held the thing up to the bulb.

I stared, soon saw them. Shrugged.

—So? If she uses it she'll get pregnant for sure.

My sibling was new to me, so I didn't understand this hatred yet.

—My mom will kill her.

I shrugged again. —Okay.

He shook his head, put it back in the box. —Her

life'll be so fucked, he laughed. My sister says all babies are assholes.

—Not all of them. I picked up five candy wrappers he'd littered on the floor, crinkled the plastic in my hand.

—Isn't she getting on your fucking nerves already? Todd asked. Doesn't she cry a lot?

—She cries sometimes, but I get up.

—Why?

I reiterated, —Because she's crying.

Todd grabbed his balls. —You sir, are a superfag.

—Your mother's a faggot, I said, looked outside. All those apartment buildings, in every direction, and so many people inside, too many for me to count.

Kids on Colden Street could sense only two things instinctively: fights and running bases. Guys sat on stoops while younger ones slapboxed for their approval. Cars were lined up and never moved. I stood in the street, raised the ball for all to see. They came at me in multitudes, like the Israelites escaping Pharaoh's bondage.

David was older, seventeen, a scourge. Normally he'd have appeared already, cut through our bodies and enthusiasm with his thick left hand, grabbed the ball from me, would have turned his back and launched that little blue globe up. It would bounce around when it hit our roof, where it would stay. Willie the Super would appear in a week with a brown box of balls: handball, football, baseball, more, that he'd sell back to us at a fair price. He and David were in on some high-class business venture. Around Flushing there were lots of ways to make money. Some harmless scheme. I even worked. One employee. Supervisor and supervised. For two dollars, you got one page. A letter, a note. You tell me the specifications and I turn out a product makes you seem: articulate, sensitive, heart-broken, serious, funny, concerned (choose one).

In my dresser drawer I had an envelope with forty-eight dollars inside, all singles. I was known for my work. Famous. Recognized by guys ages nine to nineteen as, that kid. I had been doing it for two years, since I was ten, and getting better. When I saw some guy holding hands with his new girlfriend, heard about the handjob he'd received at the movies, I took pride in knowing I had played a part. I told them all to recopy my letters in their own handwriting so females wouldn't get suspicious.

But David was not around. Munish told me, —I haven't seen him all day. When he spoke his shoulders bounced, laughter and relief.

Cindac agreed. —David hasn't fucked with us once.

We played: half a block between manhole covers, Todd and Chewy tossing the ball to each other, seven of us between them going base to base. Whoever was tagged had to throw next round. It was a long time before I went up because I was willing to run on cars. To our right was my building, six stories. Behind it, through a hole cut in the structure, was the backyard, a place of yellow weeds and broken swings. The only reason to go back there was when hiding for a game of ring-a-levio or to pop off Roman candles and block-busters.

My mother's voice came searching for me. With a job to do. She dropped a brown paper bag out the window when she found me. It floated erratically, the change inside giving it enough weight to keep from blowing into the street. —There's a list in there too, she called.

I tried to make a joke with her, but she hadn't been in the mood to laugh with me for a long time now. Grandma would try to assure me that it was too soon after having the baby for Mom to be lighthearted again, but I would see her smiling with Nabisase, even with the neighbors on our floor. Nothing as simple as an apology would smooth things. It was my fault. For so many reasons then, I turned to my sister. Everyone has their secret joys and she was mine.

Didn't check the paper until I was near the pizza parlor (one of them). Baby items. David was chilling by Lou's Diner so I spun around the back to run my errands, through the alley full of fumes.

My arms were numb by the time I'd run the last

flight of stairs, hands heavy with items in plastic bags. To the fourth floor, to our apartment door, ringing the bell with my forehead. Grandma let me pass. Mom was in the living room, flopped against the couch like she'd been punctured. The blinds were drawn; all the times my football had crashed against them had left dents and bends so that, even fully closed, slight fingers of light felt their way inside. Grandma announced my name to Mom in a whisper, as though I were being granted some audience. She worked at a grin for five minutes, then said, —Just leave those things. I'll get to them later.

—What do you need done? I asked. Is it for her? I was asking about my sister.

My mother sighed heavy, looked away from me. —I can take care of my own daughter sometimes.

I slid down onto the cushion beside Mom. My butt was already half on my sister before Mom threw out an arm and knocked me back. Nabisase lay wrapped in green, her head pointed away from the mother; her sad little cry spilled out in burps like a bottle you've tipped over. I hadn't seen her. —You sat on her. My mother laughed.

Apologized as I pulled the girl into my arms, tested around her soft spot with a gentle thumb, shook her slightly to calm her. Apologized some more.

Mom became annoyed again. —You didn't hit her with a car! Put her down. Go outside or something.

I still held her while Mom tried to put a glare on her face so I'd understand she was angry. —I'm your big brother, I said.

Nabisase was serious when she stared at me, one hand around my neck. With the other she grabbed the glasses off my face and threw them behind the couch like that should tell me something.

The next day I ran into David, his teeth so bright they seemed store-bought. I had been hiding in the backyard as, on the street, Munish counted to one hundred before starting his search for us. I was wearing skates my mother had bought me; she said they were for help- ing with my sister, a present. When I tried them on she put her hand on my back, ushered me to the door, say- ing, —You have to use those outside. They were white joints with two stripes: one red, one blue. Around my friends I felt proud rocking them, but older heads said they made me look 100-percent gay.

David had come to the backyard to smoke weed with some friend. I was behind an air-conditioning unit, the industrial kind. He pulled me from my crouch into a stand. In my skates we were about the same height. It was strange being of equal stature, so I looked down. Cindac had been hiding in some things we called bushes, when he saw me get yanked he hid harder.

—You trying to get in my business? David asked, his eyes already so red and cloudy. His face was flat and round.

—I was playing, I explained.

—Saw your ass go around me the other day, he said, blew smoke out but turned his face from me considerately. You don't want to see your friend David no more?

—I just had to get stuff for my moms, I explained.

—So? You could have said hi.

I nodded, hoping that if I agreed with him we'd keep everything cool. I didn't speak or move because I didn't want to give him anything more to discuss.

—Nice skates.

I dropped my head.

—Them's some girl's skates right? His boy managed to ask between deep hits.

I burst into an uneasy wobble. David yoked me without talking a step. I was very bad on my new skates. He dropped me quick. He leaned down, close to me, his breath warm and rich, said, —You know what I need from you?

When I wrote David's first letter I went geographical: taking her to Australia and the Great Barrier Reef, a picnic at the source of the Nile, kissing her as we leaned against the Great Wall. David wouldn't tell me who the girl was so I had to keep it all vague, no play-ing with her name, alliteration was out.

I was with Nabisase when I wrote it. She, on her back, on my bed, with her feet hefted up to her nibbling mouth and me on my stomach beside her, touched pen to the yellow legal-pad paper Mom had pilfered from work. —Should he meet her at night or daytime at the Hanging Gardens? I asked my sister.

When I spoke she darted her little black eyes at me, but only to see what was rumbling. She saw it was only her brother and looked away, to the more fascinating lightbulb, screwed into the ceiling and glowing.

Written as best the letter would ever be, I dressed Nabisase, told my mother we were going for a constitu-tional. She and Grandma were on the couch eating din-ner. They didn't agree to let me take her, but their protests were less adamant this time.

Along with us and the letter came the change of dia-pers, bottle, pacifier, bib, talcum powder, cloth, baby wipes and two comic books. As we walked I did the lit-tle mommy-bounce, the calming up and down with the girl weighted against my left hip.

We rode the elevator to the top floor, sixth. At the door to David's crib I waited and switched Nabisase to my other arm, moved the baby bag, smiled at her, kissed her baldish head. She pulled back from my lips to throw her arms at the slick, painted door. When I leaned forward to ring the bell she rested her palms against the surface. I had to ring it twice. Finally David opened up. —What?

—Letter.

He took it, turned on the light in his hallway, read it running his finger across each line, looked at me. —Nah.

—Nah?

—No.

—No? I asked. What's wrong with it?

He twisted his shoulders absently, like he was getting ready to exercise. —What I did wrong was tell you to write me a love letter. This is a love letter.

—Right.

—And I want a fuck letter.

I pulled Nabisase back like the curse was a projectile. —How I'm supposed to do that?

—You live with women, you know how they like it. Say some shit about her face. Or her ass, like that.

I wasn't going to get one decent idea from this moron; his dad was raising him alone.

—Why don't you get that for me tonight, he said.

—Tonight? I got homework.

—You think I give a fuck about your homework? He crunched the paper and threw it at me. I gotta make a diorama for fucking Art class, feel like I'm in second grade.

—I'll try.

—Try? David sneered. He stepped out of the door-

way quickfast and grabbed Nabisase. Then this motherfucker shut the door, locked it and spoke through it.
Now what the fuck you going to try?

My eyes focused on the arms, those sad loose things
that had not put up a fight. I got angry with them,
then with everything else. I kicked the door. Hard.
—Gimme back my fucking sister.

—Write the letter.

I swung the baby bag; the bottle inside popped and
popped, leaked all its milk.

—Pops isn't home, so hit that door all you want. But
if you get me mad I'ma hurt this girl.

Defeated, I said, —Then give me some paper. I'll
write it now.

Footsteps leaving, footsteps coming back; some
paper slid under the door; a pen in my jeans. I sat,
squinted as the bad lights shone down their yellow
against the yellow tiles and yellow walls until I got
dizzy. Writing, it was done in minutes.

He said, —Read it to me or I'll throw her out to the
street.

He was having fun. I imagined Nabisase going out
the window, dying on the ground, her legs snapped,
frozen at some strange angle. As big as he was, as
frightened as he made me, it wouldn't have been a
question, I'd have been through that door so easy.

I read: —You don't know how many times I've seen
you, wanted to take your hand, pull tight and look at

your face. You're so pretty it makes me mad. I want to make you forget his name and what he calls you. You think I don't really care, but what I want for you is so real.

Three locks clacked as he opened the door, handed me Nabisase, took the letter. His smile was something gentle, like he was the doctor who'd delivered my sister and now, here she is. —That's the shit, he said.

I held her close and she put one hand on each of my cheeks, a sensation I loved.

David pointed. —You write me some more shit like this. You keep it up and I won't have to bust your ass.

Me, Grandma and Nabisase went to the Botanical Gardens and parked at some benches. The old lady hadn't wanted such a large family outing. She bribed me with money to leave the two of them alone. Her English was not the greatest; as she gave me the three dollar bills she said, —You mustn't be greedy for her.

—With, I corrected. I went near the swings at the top of a hill. A tree had fallen and the way it lay, the branches and leaves came together to form a small alcove, a little cave into which you could slide, avoid overheating in the summer. I sloped toward it and peeked in for people.

David lay on his back; the girl on top of him was Michelle. They kissed heavy, her shirt up, almost off, his pants unbuttoned, hand trying extra-hard to get them down further, get his underwear off. My mouth was open, emitting a soft moan I'd have thought too low to hear over their excitement and the wind and traffic nearby, so when they bolted up, her off and over, sliding down her shirt, him buttoning his jeans, I fell backward, tumbled down the hill. I rolled on my ass and back and shoulders and neck, stopping only once I'd reached flat ground.

Grandma, dressed in blue, turned in my direction. Her friends, also old, who had gathered to witness a grandchild, who had crept from their own benches at all ends of the park, they looked at me as well. I stared up, an eye on Michelle who was tall and blond, whose long hair swung evenly like her brother's when she ran. She lifted herself over the tall black fence that surrounded the Botanical Gardens. I wondered if she was late for work. Once she was out of sight I scanned left and there he was, resting against a stone smoothed down for sitting, watching me, far enough that David's eyes were impossible to see, but from his expression I knew that I was fucked.

I wrote a letter. In it I made certain things clear, explained that courting her had just been something to do, there had been no love in it, she had just been something to try and get inside. Rough. Honest. At the bottom I signed David's name, popped it in an envelope, sealed it and walked warily down to Key Food. Todd was inside, at the gumball machine, trying to fool it with slugs. I waved the missive at him, said, —I've got something for your sister.

He nodded. —Michelle keeps everything David gives her.

I didn't say something, merely walked to register nine, slid it to her between customers. She seemed happy to receive. —This is from David? He didn't have to send me another one.

Todd and I returned to my block, raced on the sidewalk for an hour, until David appeared like out of nothing, as if me tagging the side of my building, the finish line, had been me rubbing a magic lamp to make my torturer appear like some Arabian djinn.

—What are you on, David asked, dust? Todd, suddenly, was gone.

—No, I said.

He brought his hand down on the back of my neck in the grandest of all red-necks. I fell forward into the wall, wished for my mother to open our window and scream out for me, send me to buy a thousand things, just get me far from here. But she didn't, not my grandmother either; I pictured them too busy stealing time with Nabisase while I was out, mesmerized by a hiccup while their boy came close to death.

—I knew it was stupid trusting you, he said. Now you fucked my shit all up.

Money dragged me hard by the shirt, I tripped behind him as he took me to the backyard. At the see-saws he spoke again, but his tone, he was begging; he was hurt. —Why'd you have to do that? I wasn't going to ask for no more letters. You did good. I was even going to pay you some money.

I shrugged.

—Say something! He punched me in the arm.

David wanted me to explain and he wanted me to apologize, but I wasn't sad for having destroyed his little rap. There was this routine, I knew it: two kids fuck, girl goes pregnant, belly grows, baby's born, someone goes, Mom or Dad. Kid is left with half a temple for worship; kid is left.

—You get to fuck her? I asked, thinking of her brother, Todd, and the trap he'd laid out for her just a few weeks before.

—Yeah, he said. But it wasn't even about that anymore. Then David was all over me, punching his knuckles into my thighs, pockmarking me with dead-legs. I fell backward, lay there as he hit. My throbbing was constant, seemed normal, pulsations moved up from my knees like the blood rushing through the spiraling pathways of my veins. From nearby he skipped stones at me. Some jumped off in chaotic motions while others attacked at my hands guarding my face, more tapped my ribs. When he came to me, he was not full with the joy I'd have imagined. He whispered, —It's nothing more to say to you. Every day I'm going to do this.

When I came home the television was on. I made a show at the door, shutting it forcefully, kicking my sneakers off and into the air, but they sat unperturbed. Mom and Grandma seemed to be in too good a mood to let me spoil it. A long white blanket with ruffled edges lay on the floor in front of them, lousy with trinkets: golden plastic pacifier, a set of chewable oversize plastic keys, an elephant with a wind-up trunk that whistled notes through its tusks. I went to the bathroom, washed the dirt from my face and neck, the sweat; dropped my pants and stared at the purple bruises, which were getting darker. —Where's Nabisase? I called out.

—Let her sleep, my mother yelled back. She sounded annoyed. She was also pleading.

In our room I sat on the bed and listened to the sounds my sister made as she sucked in quick, shallow breaths. She lay in her crib on her back. Even with eyes closed she looked confused, her lips parted in a little o that made her seem awestruck. I put my finger under her nose, left it there until I felt that warm in-and-out of life against my skin. Leaning on the crib made an aching noise. Every few hundred breaths her chest expanded to twice its size as she pulled in a gasp big enough for me. She moved some when this happened. I stayed, interested in the rubbery twists she managed. Moved my hand, sat it purposefully across her mouth and nose like an insect or animal feeding. I whispered, —I can't keep you safe.

The time from her last breath to the moment when she tossed her head, trying to get back to fresh air, went quickly. She was twitching, still sleeping, kicking so quickly. I held my hand there until she almost woke up, eyelids threatening to open; then I took my hand away, watched her suck in angrily but more like thankfully. Safe again, she rolled left and fell quietly back to her dreams.

My mother and grandmother wouldn't know until morning if tonight I killed her. Mom would be grateful really for no three A.M. feeding. When the sun rose she'd be one great smile, ready to handle delicately what I'd so easily destroyed. I returned my hand to her nose and mouth; as my sister's legs kicked again I listened to the light sounds she made, like newborn animals calling out for assistance in the natural order of things.

class trip

—Hookers, Willy said. You know them. You love them.

He was trying to get us interested. What do you think? He was talking to three tenth-grade boys. Fifteen years old. Among all four we didn't have half a brain. Willy, bullet-shaped head and all, was good at convincing and he wasn't even working hard.

—We are hopping on that train, he continued, heading out to Manhattan and everyone here is getting his dick sucked. No arguments.

—Who's going to put up a fight? I asked. We were each calculating how best to get some money, which parent often left a purse or wallet unguarded.

Carter asked, —How much we'll need? He stood his tall ass up in front of me. When he stretched his arms over his head Carter could run his fingers around the lip of the visible universe.

Our building was budding with age groups, men and boys. Soon someone had beer; eventually it made the rounds from the eighteen-and-ups to us and after we'd taken our pulls from the tall brown bottles there were the boys we'd once been, ten or eleven, anticipating a first taste. We could all afford such open drinking until eight or nine at night because our adults were dying at jobs. Willy never left shit to settle, so before we went off he grabbed Carter, James and me, said, —This Friday. Get like thirty dollars.

Carter and I walked, no destination, just anywhere away from home. He was chattering about where he'd get his loot, not his mother or father, but that older brother who left his cash in his old shell-toed Adidas up on a shelf in his closet. Then he asked, —So what's that woman of yours going to say about you checking out these hos?

I had forgotten about her. —Guess I won't tell, I said.

He laughed, —Man, you know you can't keep no secrets when you get drunk.

—I've never been drunk around Trisha.

Carter nodded. —Well then, maybe. He began telling me something else, he was almost whispering so it seemed like a secret. I was distracted but absently swore I heard my girl's name. I wasn't listening. It was evening in Flushing, Queens, and the buildings got glowing in that setting-sun red.

Friday, man, the whole day was full of explosive energy. During precalc a girl beside me dropped her book and in my head it sounded like a squad of soldiers battering through the door. When I saw any of the other guys we nodded conspiratorially. My girl made it easier on my conscience when she bowed out of school after third period. She clutched her belly and told me she was going home early, cramps were tearing up her insides. She had a big bag, full, and when I asked she reminded me of the trip she was taking to see her aunt, who lived in Massachusetts, some town near Boston. She'd be gone for days.

Then, in the evening, we rode the 7 out toward Manhattan. It was strange traveling with them; since about thirteen I had been coming out to wander alone. Most times I'd get off at Times Square where my ass would trip around for blocks trying to find something to kill me or make me laugh.

On the subway James scratched his balls, looked at an old asleep man, tortured in his wrinkled suit. He asked us, —What if I just punch that kid in the face? He pointed to the man. But we weren't really like that. None of us. Talk shit, that was our game. Run fast, that was our game.

—Don't start nothing, Willy said.

James sucked his teeth; the way his eyes were shaking in their sockets he seemed amped enough to hit this guy, but Willy talked him down until James sat back, sprawled out like he couldn't on his mother's couch. A year before, James got into it with an off-duty cop who was quick to show his badge and gun to James and me. The pistol was under his coat, outside his shirt, hanging on the rim of his jeans, the snubbed nose looking like a challenge. —So you're a cop, James had said. So what?

The cop was black, so I was especially scared.

—You should watch your mouth son, the cop said, though he wasn't very old himself.

James laughed that way he does, showing all his teeth; an expression that says, And?

Black Cop pressed the yellow strip to ring for his stop. In the back stairwell he said to me, —Your friend's going to get you into trouble someday.

I wasn't speaking; I nodded but my neck was soft with liquor, so I only managed a weak wobble of my head. He had made the mistake most people did, thought that because I was the quiet kid I was the one who should be saved.

———

At Times Square we discussed getting off, enjoying the flickering pleasures of video booths, but Willy was sure of his mission. He said, —Y'all will thank me when you have a mouth all on your knob.

We got off at Twenty-eighth Street, walked so quickly to the West Side Highway you'd have thought we were on wheels. A few blocks up, the Intrepid Museum was docked. I had been there three years before, with my mother and baby sister; I rode in the cockpit of a flight simulator imagining I could join the Air Force and float somewhere above the planet. James found sour balls in his jacket and sucked one.

—You keep making noises like that and some dude's going to think you're advertising, Carter said. We laughed, but then he pointed and silenced us all. There, forty feet away, was a hooker dressed all in tight silver. You can't underestimate what this meant to us; imagine Plymouth Rock.

—You suck dick? James asked. She didn't need to look up to know she should ignore us.

—Break out, she said, going through her tiny purse. She looked down the street, lit a cigarette, saw we had not left, said again, Break out.

Carter tried to make it clear. —My boy asked if you suck dick.

She whipped her red hair, real or fake, backward, elegantly. I frowned. Silver said, —You tell your boy I don't fuck with little kids. The way she switched her weight from foot one to foot two made us forget any indignation and check out her lovely hips.

—I'm saying, James charmed. I got the loot and you got the mouth, right?

Silver lost her temper, cursed at us, screamed a man's name. Then there he was, behind a rotten chain-link fence, amid these half-built homes of scavenged wood and sheets of plastic, all big shoulders and blond hair, like some *übermensch*, a fucking super-Nazi in an off-white overcoat.

Carter stayed behind to unload some more words at her; the rest of us were on the move. The expression on that guy, clearing the fence, crossing the street, was like he loved hurting people. Finally Carter appeared, stretching those long legs as he caught up to us. I looked over my shoulder, and the guy was still coming. My legs went faster. Soon I was whipping his Aryan ass like I was Jesse Owens.

The first time I held my girl's hand I was shaking so deep I couldn't control it. She looked at me. —You're shaking.

It was a strange second and I didn't say shit. This was six months before the night out with James, Willy and Carter.

Trisha said, —I think it's sweet.

We were outside school, by the library. She and I had walked out, to the October cool, because I wouldn't hold her hand in front of a crowd. —Are you that nervous? she asked.

Her hand wrapped around mine. I thought I should kiss her, touch her face, find that spot that works— opening her mouth, closing her eyes. I said, —Yeah, a little.

—Why? She was older than me. Sixteen.

—Just am.

We sat on the cold steps. She smiled. She had braces; they were shimmering and comely, there in her mouth. I had cuts across the backs of my hands. Trisha rubbed them with an open palm.

—How did these happen?

—I don't know.

—No, seriously, you can tell me these things.

I really didn't remember what had scarred them. She laughed; usually I got that reaction, laughter, from her only on the phone, where I could loosen up; in person I was always overcome by my goddamn emotions. When the cold air hit us harder, I thought of her, asked if she wanted to go in.

Trisha nodded. —It is cold. But we can stay.

I was quiet so long I forgot we were supposed to say anything.

Trisha stared to her right, to the wall where I had

played handball at nine or ten. I was very tired all the time. It didn't seem strange that I was fifteen and already feeling ancient.

She had been attached when I met her. Dating someone older, a freshman in some upstate college. He still sent her things, like bus tickets. This guy promised that if she went to him he'd give her the thing she liked most: perfume. Nice stuff I couldn't afford; all she had to do was visit. Working in my favor was distance, with its power to break bonds.

—You're quiet, I said.

She squeezed my palm. —Your hand's stopped shaking.

—You want to go to a movie? I asked quickly. We weren't dating yet, that day, just the early affection.

Her laugh came out slow so, at first, I thought she was considering it. I let go of her, asked, —What's funny?

—You should have heard yourself, she said. She squeezed her nose between two short, thin fingers, talked all nasal, You want to go to a movie?

—I sounded like that?

She touched the back of my head. —You should get a fade.

—You think so?

—I think you'd look so good with one. And, sitting like that, it was on her to lean in for the kiss. I was surprised, uncomfortable.

Then Trisha stood; I still sat, touched her feet. —They're so small.

She said, —My feet are perfect. Even the toes are nice.

I stood, laughed, liked that she was arrogant about the stupidest things.

When the four of us stopped running, Carter was the first to catch his breath, said, —Man, we could have fucked that dude up.

I punched him in the chest when I could stand straight. James and Willy heaved a minute more. We had no speed left, but we were safe. Not for the first time in our lives we were lucky.

Until a year ago none of these fellas had been my boy, but here we were looking out for one another. I went through friends quickly. That was the best thing about guys—trust comes quick and no one cries when it's over.

We walked to Twenty-seventh, where the hookers were a populace. This was their beauty: almost nothing worn, skin. We stood at a corner to watch these women move. The worst-looking one was more gorgeous than the rest of the world.

Here in the land of ass a-plenty, we were being ignored. Four black kids on foot spelled little cash and lots of hassles. These workers had no time for games.

Station wagons sped through with single passengers acting alternately calm and surprised, as though they'd found this block by accident. Husbands, fiancés and boyfriends. Newer cars bursting with twenty-year-olds eased down the street, their systems pumping heavy.

—These girls are not going to take care of us, said Willy, the pragmatist. The rest of us dreamed ideally, waved twenties at the high heels thumping past.

A woman with her glorious brown chest mostly exposed saw us, said, —Go down to Twenty-fifth.

—What's there? Willy asked.

—Crackheads. She kept walking, moving in that extra-hips way that paid her bills. The backs of her thighs were right there, platformed and performing. Exposed. It is not an exaggeration to say I would have married her that night.

We made that move. Stopped at a car, the guy inside getting a blow job. His friends were waiting, herded around a telephone, laughing. The top of a woman's head worked furiously, faster than I'd have imagined possible. I craned my neck to try and see more.

—That's Nicky! one of his friends screamed. The car window was down and Nicky inside smiled back. We rejoiced with them, but only a little, any longer and a fight might break out. They were muscle guys in zebra-print pants, leather coats; their skin looked so tough I doubted anything short of a shotgun would pierce their shells.

On Twenty-fifth the market crashed, both customers and workers. Women here wore jeans and T-
shirts like someone's fucked-up neighbor out for a
stroll. This block looked like our school's auditorium
had belched out its worst; there were slight variations
on us, in groups, canvassing the street. Truly ugly men
rode through in cars that rattled and died while waiting
at a red light, crackheads hopped into their cars two at
a time. Some rubbed close on all us boys. We tried to
act calm.

James was tired and bored. A woman appeared from
a shadowed doorway, he asked her, almost absently,
—How much for you to suck my dick?

—Fifteen.

All of us but Willy bolted upright, so sure we were
going to leave Manhattan unfulfilled. Willy stayed
shrewd. —Yeah right. He'll give you five and so will the
rest of us.

She brightened, scanned the crew. —All of you?

Willy nodded; she agreed. That was the benefit of
going to a crackhead, you could haggle.

Finally it was my turn. Carter and Willy leaned against
a building while James, just done, rubbed his stomach.
Trucks were parked on this block. Police cars seemed
to have become extinct. Occasionally you heard their
sirens bleating a few blocks up, but they seemed to

have left everything on this block for dead. Charlene ushered me down the alley she'd made into her work-place. She was about my height and twice as old. We were well hidden but she took me farther, behind a green Dumpster, lid shut.

—You know why I wanted you last, right?

I smiled. Her scalp was hidden under a blue scarf with white dots, the haphazard folds making them look as random as the salt spread out on the sidewalk after it has snowed. She kicked away the cardboard she'd laid out when taking care of my friends. I wasn't thinking of Trisha.

—I wanted the good stuff from you, she said. She brought herself close; I was not going to fuck her, no way. Get my dick sucked and move on. Then came her punches, two of them: one in the face that didn't hurt, but the second got me in the throat and I went down. On my hands and knees, this little crackhead had taken me out. The concrete was cold and one palm rested on an empty bag of chips. She was in my pock-ets, but found nothing. Then she gave me the real one, something popping against my head like a fucking brick. It was a gun.

—Get up, she said. Stand. It was the shittiest piece you'll ever see; a rusting .22, one inch above a zip gun. She was in control. Now give me that money.

No games, I got it for her. She counted out all thirty dollars, slowly, in front of me, like she was trying to rub it in. You could say I was scared, but it was delayed, didn't go off in my stomach until the four of us were catching the train an hour later and I couldn't ease my token into the slot; Carter took it from my palsied hand and pushed me through.

—You robbed them all? I asked.

—Nope. Just you.

—Why me?

She put the money away, scratched at her pussy from outside her jeans. My head was bleeding. I saw that she was peeing her pants before I smelled it; the stain spread in her crotch and soon the thin yellow slacks were loosing droplets that fell to the ground between her and me. She answered my question. —I don't like your face, she said. You just don't look good.

The whole next week in school I was hoping for my girl's return, but Trisha was out for five days. I'd call her at home. One of her older sisters would only take a message, firmly say she'd call me, but the next night I dialed the number. I felt guilty, spent hours considering how much better life would be if I'd stayed out of the alley, if I'd been a better man.

Finally Trisha appeared. We went out to dinner. She sat at the table warm in her jacket and a turtleneck. She held my hand when we walked, but swatted me off when I tried to kiss her neck. This diner was good: the seats squeaked when you slid into a booth and a small cup of coleslaw came with every meal. —Tonight, she said, I'm paying.

—I won't argue with that.

She laughed. —You never have a problem with spending my money.

—I was going to buy you something, I told her.

She sipped her water. We were quiet until a waiter came trolling for orders.

She asked, —Where is it?

—I didn't have enough, I admitted.

—Yeah, I know you. You spent that money on nonsense.

I smiled. —You got that right beautiful.

—So what was it?

A group came into the diner and in the wonderful anonymity of the American family, I thought they'd just left. —Look. I pointed. Trisha peeped them, but wasn't into laughing at stability. I was going to get you this bear.

—A teddy bear?

The food arrived. —Don't say it like that, I protested. It was a nice one. Had a smoking jacket and a pipe. He looked like me. Don't you think he would be cute?

She ate. Dinner done, she paid the bill. We got up and out. Flushing at night was like Flushing during the day, just darker. Together we walked to her building.

—Anyone ever ask why you're dating a younger man?

—Maybe.

She wore a new good smell applied to her skin, but I ignored it, busy instead rubbing my nose, my chin, my neck, learning my face's true dimensions.

—And what did you tell him?

She shrugged. —What should I have said?

We walked fast. Soon her building stood before us. It wasn't so big but tonight it seemed majestic. Trisha's two older sisters were outside. —Hey Anthony, Gloria said, looking to the others. The secrets this bunch held among them were enough to destroy one thousand ex-boyfriends. Trisha smiled, waited.

—What? I asked.

—You aren't going to thank me for paying?

—You're right. Thank you so much. The food was delicious.

—I know. She touched my side.

—Am I ugly? I asked her.

—You? She put her face against my neck. She tried to tickle me but neither of us was laughing. On the street, traffic was still a thriving business; the sky was purple and lost.

acknowledgments

More important than anything or one, I'd like to thank my wonderful family: to Kezia Kanyike, Christopher Kanyike and Shana LaValle, you three have helped to raise this man. To James LaValle, I think of you as well. Paul LaValle who always represents. Hileria LaValle who is kind, beautiful and good. Chris Seninde, Rebecca Bain and their families have always been loving and supportive. To Damali, Namutebi and the Seninde family in Uganda. Thanks also to Jessica Kazina.

These are my peoples, I owe you each: Eric Gluck, the Gluck Family, Rob Farley, Ramon M. Gonzalez III

acknowledgments

(I know, this isn't even one line), Tyrone Martinez-Black, Ms. Martinez, Akira Bryson, the Bryson Family, Ashanti Dawson, Zai Collier, the Collier Family, Rahsaan "Rocky" Robinson, Roy Clovis, Krishna Collie, Andres Hernandez, Nate Williams, Roberto Garcia, Nina Cooke, Scott Ruff, Camilla Hayes and Lisette Belliard. More recently Mat Johnson, Doug Jones, Myron Hardy, Andrea Green, Julie Nichols, Joanna Hershon, the great Peter Shen and Valerie Roche.

The title of this collection is a sample from a line in "Daytona 500" by Ghostface Killah. In three words a good poet captured what took me two hundred pages.

Heather Clay, I am in your debt for having made this book possible (truly).

Thanks to Junot Díaz for giving me my best writing lesson early on: that we could write about ourselves.

Jennie Smith. Your work keeps teaching me what more a writer can accomplish. Can I embarrass you? Every time I think you're the greatest, you get better.

I was fortunate enough to have four magnificent writing teachers: thanks to Rebecca Goldstein for championing the love of writing, Helen Schulman for forcing my stories to tell a story before anything else, Maureen Howard for precision, a careful eye on the manuscript and of course, a leg up. And Michael Cunningham for energetic praise, tireless support and genuine inspiration.

Deb Treisman of *The New Yorker* for such interest, heartfelt support and kind words.

BOMB magazine, specifically Suzan Sherman and Minna Proctor for being the first ones to take a chance on anything in here.

Gratitude to Marion Ettlinger for taking a great picture and making me feel so fine while working. Let's make a pilgrimage back to Flushing.

Special praise to the Fine Arts Work Center in Provincetown, a boon to any writer who takes his work seriously. I am indebted to you for the time, the space and, oh yeah, the money.

Jenny Minton, you must have read this a thousand times. Thanks for helping me to push, pull, punch and primp this book into what we'll show the world.

Adam Pringle, permissions king. Tireless. You are owed many, many drinks.

Immense gratitude to Rob Hewitt and to Marty Asher, Katy Barrett, Susie Leness, David Hyde, Philip Patrick, Anne Messitte, Mark Maguire, and Suvi Asch at Vintage Books for working so earnestly and with such excitement to get this book out to the public, to make my work worthwhile.

Aaron Hamburger for your performance and help early on.

To Katherine Fausset for your concern, appreciation and supportive words at the end of those rejection letters.

Lastly thanks to superagent Gloria Loomis for loving this collection, being its most vocal advocate and for your belief in me.

31901046430270